BUTTONS & BURGLARY

A CRAFT AND GHOST COZY MYSTERY

A DRESS DESIGNER COZY MYSTERY SERIES

LUCINDA RACE

MC TWO PRESS

Editor Trish Long @ Blossoming Pages
Cover design by Molly Burton of
CozyCoverDesigns.com

Manufactured in the United States of America
First Edition July 2025

Print Edition ISBN 978-1-966424-27-7
Print Large Print ISBN 978-1-966424-28-4
Print Hard Cover ISBN 978-1-966424-36-9
E-book ISBN 978-1-966424-25-3

1. Town Hall
2. Lillith Park
3. Grants Gowns
4. Whistlers Inn
5. Twice Loved
6. DB Pharmacy
7. Drakes Bay Bank
8. Police Department
9. Knit or Purl
10. 5 Cents a Dance
11. Polly's Pantry
12. Brewed Bliss
13. Blossoms on the Bay
14. Scoop-a-licious

1

QUICK NOTE: If you enjoy Buttons & Burglary, check out my offer for a FREE novella at the end. With that, happy reading.

I settled into a deck chair savoring the warm afternoon, the view of Drakes Bay, and a glass of lemonade on the side table. Then my cell phone pinged. It was

Beth, the owner of Knit or Purl and my new best friend.

Be over in ten. Bringing appetizers.

I grinned. Dinner alfresco sounded perfect after the day I'd had. One issue after another arose, not with my brides but with their mothers. It was time to put the day behind me. I glanced at my watch and saw I still had time to call about the antique buttons. Twice Loved, the second-hand shop in town, was open. I dialed and waited for Fiona Doyle to answer.

"Hello, Twice Loved."

"Hi, Fiona. It's Claudia Grant."

"Hello. This is a surprise. I didn't expect to hear from you until Sunday. You're still coming for dinner, aren't you?"

"I'm looking forward to it." It had been a standing monthly invitation that my late Uncle Herman and Fiona had. When I first moved to town and discovered his ghost was lingering, he asked if I'd continue to have dinner with his old friend.

"Excellent. What can I do for you tonight?"

"I worked with a bride today. She asked me to refresh her grandmother's wedding dress, which was missing buttons. I hoped to look through your button boxes to see if I could find some that would match or at least complement the dress."

"Of course. Recently, I purchased a box at an auction. If you'd like to come over now, I can unpack it. I don't mind staying open a little later."

"No, thank you. I don't want you to go to any trouble tonight, but if I could look on Sunday, that would give me plenty of time to devise a new plan if nothing would work."

"Absolutely. I'll check to make sure I don't have any other boxes tucked away. Sometimes, I squirrel away fun do-dads to peruse on a rainy day."

"Great." Now that business was settled, I

asked, "Would you like me to bring anything special for dessert on Sunday?"

"Whatever you'd like." She giggled like a schoolgirl. "I've never met a sweet I didn't enjoy."

"Then it will be a surprise."

"Goodbye, Claudia. See you soon, and don't forget to come hungry."

She disconnected, and I smiled. Herman had been right when he said Fiona was wonderful. Personally, I think he had a crush on the woman and was too shy to speak up. But that ship sailed.

I went inside my apartment. "Lola, time for dinner." The sweet Himalayan cat thumped into the kitchen and jumped on the table. She stared at me.

"Did I interrupt your nap, little lady?" A breeze slid over my arm. "Herman. You've made yourself scarce today."

"That woman, the bride's mother, Mrs. Vanderkemp, is insufferable. I couldn't listen to another minute of her moaning about re-making that hideous dress—her words, not mine."

"Julia is sweet, and the dress isn't that bad, despite what her mother thinks." He was right. I didn't have a bridezilla on my hands; I had a MOB-zilla. "It'll be beautiful when I'm done with it."

"I'm sure it will. You're quite talented, but the best part of being a ghost is that I no longer have to deal with customers like her."

I laughed. "You're a resident ghost with strong opinions. How did I get so lucky?"

He frowned. "I should have crossed over to where I'm meant to live for eternity after you found out how I died. I believe you're stuck with me forever."

"There are worse fates than hanging out with me." I opened a can of food for Lola and set the plate on the table, giving her ears a quick scratch. I had given up trying to convince her that cats ate their food on the floor.

A good scrub of the table was all that was needed when she was finished. At least she didn't get on the table all the time, just for meals.

"You're right. Don't you wonder why I'm still here?"

"Unfinished business, I suppose." I poured a glass of lemonade for Beth and placed it on a tray with small plates and napkins.

If a ghost could sigh, Herman did before he drifted from the kitchen. I knew he would take his usual spot on the window ledge in the living room, look down the street, or make his way to the dress shop.

I was about to comfort him when I heard Beth call to me.

"Claudia, are you coming out?"

I picked up the tray and walked to the door. Pushing the screen with my hip, I stepped onto the deck. "Your timing is perfect. I've fed Lola, and it's time to put our feet up."

She placed a tray overfilled with finger foods on the table between the lounge chairs and reclined. "It's been a day. Is there a full moon tonight? I swear every customer was out to push my buttons."

"Same." I set my tray on the dining table and passed her the lemonade, plate, and a napkin. "I had a MOB-zilla."

She wrinkled her nose. "What's that?"

"A mother of the bride who's acting like Godzilla."

"I get it now. Someone local?"

I eased into the chair after filling a small plate. "No, that's the funny part. They're from New Hampshire. I never thought anyone would drive a long distance to my little dress shop. Despite that, the mother of the bride is lovely, and I can't wait to design dresses for the two attendants."

"You possess a unique talent for making people feel beautiful when they wear one of your designs. It's truly a special gift."

Heat flushed my cheeks. "Thank you. I— I don't know what to say."

She held up her glass. "Cheers to us. We survived our customers and a long day. Tomorrow will be easier."

With a laugh, our glasses clinked together. "Salute."

I leaned back. "I can't believe it's been six months since I moved to Drakes Bay. Living in Maine is a dream come true."

"After the rocky start, the sofa sleuths started strong, but since we solved the murder of Colton Prescott and Herman's death, life's returned to normal. Well, except for the summer tourists."

"I think we should leave solving crimes to your cousin, Eddie." I sipped my drink, hoping to avoid her questioning look. I tried hard not to show anyone that I thought he was the best thing since the invention of the sewing machine and oh-so sigh-worthy.

"He's not dating anyone. Why don't you

ask him out? The fall festival in Pembroke Cove is coming up soon."

"I have too much that requires my attention. The business is more than a full-time job."

She snorted. "Right. We could go to the festival if you want. It's a lot of fun; you'll see Lily and Gage again. She always has a booth with her parents' tea for sale."

"That sounds like fun."

With a saucy wink, she said, "I'll ask Eddie to come with us. Just as a friend for you, of course."

I shook my head. Eager to change the subject, I cleared my throat. "The dress I'm going to remake is missing some buttons. Do you have anything in your shop that could be considered antique knockoffs?"

"Stop in before we open tomorrow, and I'll let you look around. But Fiona's store would be a better option."

"She mentioned that I could view her inventory on Sunday when I'm there for dinner. However, I don't have high hopes of finding what I need. Having a backup plan could help me avoid a trip to Boston or New York City. I'm sure I could find what I'd like there, but I'd prefer not to waste the time driving."

"I have button books available for you to check out, and ordering through me can help you save money. What about your inventory?"

"Nothing will work. I've already checked the basement where Herman kept old lace and leather. He didn't collect buttons."

We nibbled in silence.

"Herman was a terrific guy. I wish you could have met him."

I spoke to his ghost every day and likely knew him as well as I would have if he were alive. "I feel like I know him after everything you and your dad have shared. Fiona's filled in some gaps, too."

"That's good." She pulled out her phone. "Hold on, it's Eddie." She pressed a button on her cell. "Hey, cuz, what's up?" With a nod, she smiled. "We were just talking about that." Pause. "I'll ask her and get back to you, but it sounds great." Another pause. "Talk soon." She grinned. "You'll never guess what Eddie wanted."

With a chuckle, I said, "You can tell me, and we'll both know."

"Eddie asked if we wanted to go with him and Luke Devlin to the Pembroke Cove Fall Festival next Saturday."

"Did you set this up?"

She waved a hand at me. "Innocent. But this indicates that Eddie wants a reason to spend time with you, and Luke is adorable." With a wink, she laughed. "I can endure his company for an afternoon."

"Sounds more like a date for you two and we're making plans ten days in advance?"

"Correct. It will give us plenty of time to find something to wear."

"I'm guessing both guys know what you look like, and Eddie has spent time around me, so why go through all the trouble of picking outfits?"

"Well, if Eddie doesn't trip your trigger, then maybe you'll meet someone else, so you need to look nice. But I'm sure he's got a thing for you."

I shook my head. "I try to always look decent."

She patted my arm. "Claudia, you wear black or navy almost every day while working. It's time to put a lot of color in your wardrobe."

"I have color." My thoughts drifted to my closet, and she was right; most of it was monochromatic. But I had nine days to whip up a new top that I could pair with jeans.

"It might be cool, so you'll want a nice sweater. I have the perfect one at the store. I finished it last night and planned to wear it, but you can try it first."

"You're determined to increase the contents in my sweater drawer."

"If we continue to support each other

with our talents, we'll have the best wardrobes in town."

"And we'll be walking advertisements for our stores." I raised my hand for a high five.

"Women businesses working together is our superpower."

"It is." Darkness crept across the bay. "I know I haven't told you, but I'm happy we're friends. You made the transition much easier."

"I know what you mean." She clasped my hand. "Even if we never have to be sofa sleuths again, we've got each other's backs in every aspect of life, and I'm fortunate you moved to town. Making good friends has been difficult for me. The girls at school thought I was odd growing up because I loved to knit."

I understood exactly what she meant. "Sewing wasn't exactly popular, either."

Getting to her feet, Beth stretched her arms over her head. "Look at us now. Forging our destinies with amazing businesses in a charming coastal town. What more could we ask for in life?"

I couldn't think of anything. "Antique buttons?" I chuckled. "If that's my biggest challenge this week, aside from MOB-zilla, I'm a happy seamstress."

It was nine the next morning when I crossed the street to Knit or Purl. The door was propped open, and I went in. "Beth?"

I heard a muffled response that sounded like "In the office."

Wandering through the yarn shop had become a favorite pastime. I hesitated but contemplated picking up a beginner set of needles and yarn. Every set was designed for children, but my foolish pride held me back each time.

"Morning." Beth emerged from the back room, holding several magazines. "I brought my accessory catalogs for you to take with you." She set them on the counter. "First, let's look at a few options on the rack."

I walked with her as she guided me to the back wall. "You never said if the buttons were covered, metal, or wood."

"The buttons might have been ivory colored or pearl and secured with a loop, so there are no buttonholes."

She nodded. "Then what I have here won't work. I don't have any ivory buttons in stock. I thought maybe there were covered buttons, and I do have that option, since I've used them as a base for crocheted buttons."

"Is there any end to your talent with yarn?"

She laughed. "I hope not. I keep pushing myself to learn new techniques and styles."

I scanned the rack, but nothing caught my eye. "I'll take the books. After I look at Fiona's stock, I'll figure out my next step."

"Just tell me how I can help."

The door opened. The bell above it jingled as Ethan walked in. "Good morning, ladies."

"Hi, Dad. Did you stop at Brewed Bliss?"

He held up a paper bag and cardboard tray. "As requested." His smile grew. "Good morning, Claudia."

"Hi, Ethan. How's things?"

"Good. I just chatted with Chief Durgin, and he mentioned that Barbara Hall and Amos Branson took a plea deal, and he wanted me to pass along his thanks for the details you provided."

"That took a long time." I took the coffee he held out to me.

"Not really. It takes time to bring people to trial, and during the waiting period, I think Barbara and Amos thought about what happened and decided not to fight the inevitable."

"Sadly, money ruined lives," Beth said.

"Look at the bright side. It brought us together. If we hadn't dived into the world of Nancy Drew and Bess, who knows what might have happened."

Ethan went behind the counter and set the

bag down. "Not bad for your first and last case."

Beth said, "It was fun, even if it was a little scary."

I gave her a wink. "We could come out of retirement if necessary."

2
____

made my way to the bay side of Twice Loved. Fiona had a set of outdoor stairs, like mine, leading to her apartment. I carried a box of pink iced chocolate cupcakes and a pint of Butter Brickle ice cream from Scoop-a-Licious. I discovered it's worth the extra stop for sharing a decadent dessert with Fiona.

I rapped on the screen door and turned to take in the view of the bay. It was something I'd never get tired of looking at. A faint groan reached my ears. I spun around and hurried to the door.

"Fiona?" I hesitated to walk in.

I heard a weak voice say, "Help."

This time, I didn't hesitate. Flinging open the door, I set the dessert and shoulder bag on the inside bench. "Fiona, where are you?"

The door to her shop was wide open. My heart was in my throat, praying I wouldn't find her at the bottom like Herman had been discovered. I raced down the steps. When I reached the last step, I called again. "Fiona?"

"Over here."

The shop was filled with shadows, remnants from the afternoon sun. I scanned each aisle. "Where?"

"Front."

The word was weaker than before. "I'll be right there." I raced down the nearest aisle and fell to my knees. Fiona lay in front of the door, her body crumpled in a way I hadn't thought possible for the human form. Could she have broken bones?

I clasped her hand. "Where does it hurt?"

"My head and shoulder."

"I'm going to call for help."

She clung to my hand. "Don't. Leave. Me."

"I'm going to stay with you, but I need to call the police, and my phone is upstairs. Can I step out for a minute?"

"All right."

It was a miracle that I heard her. I retraced my steps, opened my bag, and dialed the phone while running down the stairs for the second time.

A male voice said, "9-1-1. What's your emergency?"

"This is Claudia Grant. I'm at Twice Loved. Fiona Doyle has been attacked. Can you send an ambulance?"

"Is there an intruder?"

An icy shiver slithered down my spine. Were we alone? "I'm not sure."

"Please stay on the line until emergency personnel arrive."

"Okay." I sank to my knees once more and

took Fiona's hand. "Everything will be fine. Help is on the way."

Her eyes fluttered closed.

I pressed my fingertips to her wrist. There was a steady, albeit faint, pulse. "Fiona, open your eyes and look at me."

"It hurts my head." She shivered. "I'm so cold."

I looked around. A few steps away, a quilt was artfully draped over a chair. "I'll get something to cover you."

I placed the blanket over her and took her hand in mine.

"Claudia, what's happening?" the operator asked.

"Fiona's cold, and she keeps closing her eyes."

"You've covered her with a blanket?"

"Yes."

"Keep talking to her."

"Fiona, this nice man on the phone says I must continue talking to you. So please, open your eyes." The wail of a siren grew louder. "Do you hear that?"

Her eyes fluttered again. "Yes."

"I have to let them in, but I promise you're safe, and I won't leave you." Reluctant to let go of her hand, I waited until I saw someone at the door. Stepping around her, I twisted the deadbolt and pulled it open.

Eddie strode in. "Claudia, what happened?"

I stumbled back against a shelf. He reached out a hand to steady me. "It's okay. We're here."

I nodded. He pushed the door open wide so the two EMTs could come inside. They each carried rigid plastic boxes, which I assumed contained vital supplies.

"When I got here, well upstairs, I knocked on the door. Fiona didn't answer right away. We're having dinner tonight."

He nodded. "Go on." His hand rested on my shoulder.

"I knocked a second time and called out

to her. That's when I heard a groan. Then, 'Help.' I rushed inside and saw the door open to her shop." I blinked away hot tears. "I was so scared I'd find her at the bottom of the stairs."

Eddie maintained comforting and steady eye contact. "I understand. Did you see anyone when you came inside?"

Shaking my head, I said, "No. I was focused on Fiona."

"Okay. Then what happened?"

"I found her like that. I didn't move her, but I called for help." My mouth dropped open. "Wait, I forgot to tell the operator that you're here."

I put the phone to my ear. "Hello."

"I'm still here. Have the police and ambulance arrived?"

"Yes. Thank you."

"You're in good hands." He disconnected.

Eddie steered me to a chair. "We should give the EMTs room to work."

Allowing him to remove me from the immediate area was nerve-wracking. "I promised Fiona I wouldn't leave her."

"You haven't, but the professionals need room, and it's in short supply."

Standing on my tiptoes, trying to see over or around Eddie, I called to her. "Fiona, I'm right over here."

I saw she lifted a couple of fingers, and I took that as an acknowledgment.

Eddie said, "Take a deep breath. Each time, concentrate on your breath, in through your nose and out through your mouth."

While I did as he asked, I scanned the room. "Fiona must have interrupted an intruder." I grasped his forearm. "We have to look upstairs. If they're still here, they can't get away."

"Whoever it was is long gone. If they had been here when you arrived, they would have snuck out when you were distracted."

He made a good point. "But we'll search it once Fiona goes to the hospital?"

"The police will conduct a search. You will not."

"I can help." I tipped my head to the table to the left of where Fiona lay, which was empty. "That's odd."

Eddie turned to see what I was looking at. "What?"

"Look around. Except for that mahogany table, every surface is covered with boxes, books, and trinkets. It's strange."

"Fiona must have sold something and not replaced it yet."

I shook my head. "No. She'd never leave a spot open. Each time I've been in the shop, the moment a customer leaves with something, she rearranges items so there isn't a bare space. She believes customers expect each surface to be overflowing, stimulating impulse buys since people can't resist picking up items while wandering around the store."

His brow arched. "Any idea what might have been there?"

Narrowing my eyes, I tried to recall what

might have existed in that space. "Other than the fact that it was square, I don't have a clue." Fiona was being lifted onto a gurney. "I'll be right back."

She held out her hand. "Claudia, would you mind locking my apartment and the shop when the police are done? And tell them I have no idea who assaulted me."

I took her hand. "Eddie Jacobs is here. He's going to give the place a thorough going over. Try not to worry about anything. I'll come to the hospital as soon as he's finished."

"You don't need to do that." A tear slipped from the corner of her eye. "It would be comforting to have a friend by my side."

Giving her hand one last squeeze, I offered her a reassuring smile. "I'll be there the moment I lock up."

"Thank you." She turned her head and nodded to Eddie. "Take care of everything."

"No need to worry, Ms. Doyle." He stepped closer. "You don't have any idea who assaulted you?"

"No. I had been puttering around down here. I went upstairs to unlock the door and heard a crash, so I returned to look around, and someone approached from behind me."

"Do you know what time that was?"

"I think around four," she closed her eyes.

An older man, whom I estimated to be around forty, nodded. "Eddie, we need to get her to the ER."

"Right." He moved in front of the gurney and held the door.

I wanted to encourage Fiona, but I was at a loss for words. They put the stretcher in the back of the ambulance, and the same man got in next to her. Beth was running in our direction.

"What's going on?" She looked at me and then Eddie. "Was that Fiona?"

Nodding, I pulled her inside the store. I didn't want anyone to overhear us. Eddie closed the shop door after him.

"What's happened?"

Eddie said, "This is an official police investigation."

She stamped her foot. "Eddie Jacobs, stop being all tough cop on me. Fiona is on her way to the hospital, and you're here. Which means she didn't slip and fall. What gives?"

"I'll tell you what I know."

Eddie said, "I'm going to wait for additional officers to gather evidence."

"I knew it. Is Fiona going to be okay?"

"She was attacked, but she was talking when the EMTs took her to the ER. That's a good sign."

She nodded. "It is. Why would someone hurt Fiona? She's a sweet woman."

"I think there's been a break-in. Take a look." I led her to the empty table. "You know how particular Fiona is about her displays; she would never leave a space vacant on any surface at the end of the day."

Frowning, she said, "I can't think what she had here."

"Neither can I. It was something small

enough to fit in a backpack." I tapped my finger to my lips. "You take the right side of the room, and I'll handle the left. Look for anything that seems out of place."

"You mean as if something was picked up and placed on another table?"

I nodded. "Yes. Perhaps I'm jumping to conclusions about a situation that hasn't occurred. Fiona might have opted to rearrange her inventory before she opens tomorrow."

Beth's one eyebrow arched. "Unlikely, but let's check it out."

Eddie was on the sidewalk in front of the store. "He must have gone around the back." A police cruiser pulled up, and a female officer stepped out

"Who's that?" I watched her as she gave Eddie a half smile before her expression became blank. "She's pretty."

"If you like petite brunettes proficient in martial arts and sharpshooting." Beth stood next to me, watching the exchange. "Rhonda

Perkins, a new cop. Eddie told us she moved here from Camden."

With a low whistle, I said, "Seems she's interested in Eddie."

Beth gave me a sharp look. "She doesn't stand a chance in Hades with him. He'd never date another cop or any public servant. It could get messy. Rumor has it that's why she left her last job. Broke up with a boyfriend who was also on the force."

"Makes sense. Blurring those lines could be career ending."

He bobbed his head to the door. She nodded.

"They're coming in." I didn't want it to look like we were being nosy, so I strolled out of view of the door. Beth giggled, but she was right behind me. They came in, and he glanced my way.

"Eddie, did you find anything outside the back door?"

He gave me a somber look. "It was jimmied open. We'll need to dust for prints inside the store and on the door.

"It was a break-in." I spoke more under my breath than out loud.

Officer Perkins asked, "Who are you?"

Eddie said, "My cousin, Beth Stewart, and her friend, Claudia Grant. She owns Grants Gowns two doors down. Ladies, this is Officer Rhonda Perkins."

"And why are you roaming around our crime scene?"

I didn't appreciate the condescending tone in her voice or the implication that I didn't belong here. "Fiona and I were planning on sharing a meal, and I discovered her."

"Claudia, Officer Jacobs and I don't need civilians contaminating our crime scene. You can leave now."

Eddie said, "I've asked them to look around the store and see if they notice anything out of place. Claudia and Beth are frequent visitors to Twice Loved."

I stood straighter as Eddie defended us. "Not to worry. We know not to touch anything, and if we discover something, we'll tell Eddie immediately."

"Now that I'm here, you can advise me."

Was this officer trying to assert herself? What was it with cops and having an attitude? I smiled. "I'd be happy to keep you informed." Turning abruptly, I bumped into Beth. Her eyes widened, and a glint of mischief sparkled. "Come on. The sooner we look around, the quicker we can leave."

I snapped my fingers. "Shoot. I left the ice cream on the bench upstairs." Glancing over my shoulder, I caught Eddie's eye. "Is it okay if I run upstairs and put the ice cream in the freezer?"

With a nod, he said, "I'll come with you. I have a few questions."

Beth said, "I'll stay here and keep looking for clues."

Officer Perkins said, "You're not looking

for clues. You're providing me with in-formation."

I smothered a laugh when Beth looked at me and rolled her eyes out of Rhonda's line of sight. "I'll be right back."

"Take your time."

As I walked away, Beth asked, "Claudia, how big would you say the missing item would be?"

I glanced at the table once more. "It's approximately a twelve-inch square box. It could be made of wood, metal, or plastic."

She gave a brisk nod. "Got it."

I climbed the stairs slowly; I examined each tread using my cell phone flashlight.

"I've already done that. They're clean—not even a dust bunny."

"I wouldn't expect anything less from Fiona, but you never know."

When I reached the top step, I was in her apartment. Its layout was like mine, and the afternoon sun warmed the room. "Where do you want to start?"

Eddie gestured to the door. "Walk me through what happened when you arrived, and we can look around."

I shot him a sharp glance. "Don't let your coworker know you're supporting me in searching for clues."

"Not clues. Evidence. There's a difference. You have an excellent eye for detail; why not take advantage of it?"

I walked to the back door, and we walked onto the deck. "I came up the steps and knocked on the door. Fiona didn't answer right away, so I enjoyed the view." For authenticity, I reenacted my movements. "I knocked again and called out to her. This time, I thought I heard a groan. I opened the door," which I did again, "and placed the box and pint down along with my bag." I bent over like I was doing it. Tipping my head, I said, "Eddie, by chance, did you eat a cupcake?"

"When? Today?"

I pointed to the box and said, "There were four. One is missing."

3

Eddie stopped me before I could grab the box. "Claudia. Wait. Are you sure there were four cupcakes?"

I popped my hands on my hips. "I just bought them before I came over. If you don't believe me, ask Sue at Brewed Bliss."

He hung his head. "I wasn't doubting you. It's just that it's over the top for someone to break in, assault an older woman, presumably steal something from the store, and then take a cupcake. Maybe we'll catch a break and there'll be fingerprints."

Feeling the color drain from my face, I grabbed his arm and took a deep, ragged breath. "Whoever hurt Fiona was in the building when I arrived. They know about me, and what if they think I saw them? Will they come after me next?" Ice encased my heart as the beating slowed. I sank to the bench.

Eddie knelt beside me. "In my expert opinion, if they believed you had seen them, they would have attempted to harm you while trying to escape. Instead, they waited until you rushed down to help Fiona, grabbed a cupcake, and then fled."

Nodding, he spoke logical and comforting words. "I was so focused on Fiona that I was oblivious to everything else." I clutched his hand, knowing I had already said it, but the events had shaken me to my core so I repeated myself. "I expected to find her at the bottom of the stairs."

"Like Herman?"

"Yes." The word was barely a whisper. I

took several deep breaths before straightening my spine. I wouldn't let this deter me from figuring out what happened here. Not that I'd tell Eddie about my plan. With Beth already poking around downstairs and me upstairs, the whiteboard would soon come out of the closet and be put to good use.

My brow furrowed. "If Fiona said she heard a noise at four and I arrived at five, then the person took their time searching the place." I stood. "We need to walk through the apartment. Whoever it was might have left clues up here, too."

He grinned. "And just like that, you're back. We'll walk through the apartment together, but don't touch anything."

"Can I have a pair of gloves?"

"Um. No. That is official police work. Gloves are not for civilian use."

"Spoilsport." I hoped he'd catch the sass in my words. I had a moment of panic, but now I had returned to normal, and my brain was in overdrive.

He chuckled. "I've never met a girl as curious about investigating as you."

"Except your cousin?"

"Only since you moved to town." He pointed to the hall. "We should start with the bedrooms."

"Most likely, that's where the intruder hid when I came in." I slipped my hands into my pockets to avoid the temptation of touching anything.

Eddie smiled. "Good idea. I don't want to explain why your fingerprints are everywhere since it's common knowledge Fiona loves to polish every surface." He donned a pair of gloves.

"How come you don't have detectives to do this kind of thing? You're a regular cop, right?"

"We're a small team. With Rhonda joining us and based on my experience, I feel ready to take on the role of a detective."

"Like a hybrid position?" I strolled past a side table in the hall, which didn't have drawers or doors, so it was undisturbed.

"Yes." He pushed open the door to a small guest bedroom. A petite desk stood on the far side of the room. The drawers were open, and their contents littered the floor. "Bingo."

"This is a bit of a mess." I crossed the room and had the itch to tidy the space but didn't.

"They must have searched here because they didn't find what they were looking for downstairs."

Shaking my head, I said, "I disagree. They took something from that table. Fiona wouldn't have left that space open. I'll ask her when I get to the hospital."

"No. You won't question the victim. That's a matter for the police."

"Can I be in the room when you talk to her?"

"Claudia." He shook his head. "Can't we play by the rules?"

"She's been through a lot today. Answering numerous questions might be diffi-cult for her, considering she was attacked in a place she thought was safe."

He was taking pictures with his phone, and I did the same before he answered my last question. I had no idea what I was looking at, but if Eddie felt it was necessary, it made sense for me to follow his lead.

"Hey, what's that smeared on the paper? Could it be grease from a shoe?"

He knelt on the floor. "It's a smudge of dirt. It could be nothing, but there might be trace evidence. We'll send it to a lab in Port-land to be analyzed." He glanced my way and nodded. "Good eye."

"See? I'm an asset." Without waiting for him to respond, I gave the pile of papers a wide berth and crossed to the open window. "No screen. Isn't that odd?" I glanced at the deck outside. "Eddie, it's been removed. This was either a way to enter or exit."

"They didn't come in this way. The back door was ajar. Thinking like the perp, he planned to go out this window and down the emergency ladder until you showed up. Then, they changed course and slipped out the main door."

"Why go through the trouble of pushing the screen out?"

"The main back stairs can be seen from the beach. I'm sure the emergency stairs are located closer to the alley. We'll check when we finish up here."

I took a bunch of pictures that I was sure wouldn't be helpful before walking back into the hall and turning into Fiona's bedroom. It overlooked Main Street and the food market. This room looked untouched. The dresser drawers weren't open, and the closet doors were latched. I wandered into the adjoining bath. It also looked pristine.

"Eddie, the intruder must have found what he was looking for in the other room."

"Agreed. We'll look around the living room and kitchen and then for the emergency ladder."

We toured the apartment, and I took photographs of each room. From my observations, someone had searched the shop and the spare room—which must serve as Fiona's office. "I'm going to put the cupcakes in the refrigerator and the ice cream in the freezer."

He extended his hand to stop me from walking toward the entrance. "I have to take them into evidence." He nodded at the ice cream. "You might want to toss that."

Playfully, I asked, "Are you sure you don't need to take that too?"

"If he had been interested in the pint, he would have taken it with him since he wasn't concerned about removing the cupcake. I hope he left a print on the box."

"I'll take the ice cream when I leave. I don't want it sitting in Fiona's trash; it'll make a mess."

Pushing open the screen door, he ushered me outside. First, I walked to the screen lying on the deck. "Can we put this back in?"

"Not yet. I'll come back and dust it for prints."

I peered over the edge to where the fire stairs hung; they graced the ground near a garbage dumpster. "We have to leave this as is, too?"

"For now. Before Fiona comes home, I'll ensure everything is back in its proper place."

"Thank you. That's very kind."

We walked down the main stairs, when we reached the bottom, I turned away from the beachside entrance and walked down the alley between the store and the inn.

"You were right. From this vantage point, whoever came down the ladder could have stayed behind the dumpster without being seen before walking to the street. Sneaky perp."

"Most are." Eddie took another series of pictures, and I followed suit. "You do realize that I know you've been taking lots of pictures. But I want you and Beth to stay out of this investigation. He attacked an older woman and left her bleeding on the floor. Who's to say he wouldn't have an issue hurting either of you if he thought you were trying to ferret out the truth?"

"For one thing, we're like forty years younger. It would be more difficult for the attacker to get the jump on us, and you forget I was able to disarm not one but two people who were threatening my life."

"You got lucky, and my uncle helped a little."

"I was there, remember?" I suppressed the shudder, thinking how it could have turned out very badly for Ethan and me. I snapped a few pictures. "What's next?"

"I see what you did—diverting the conversation." He nodded toward the direction we had come from. "We should go back to the shop. I'll check in with Rhonda, and you can see if Beth discovered anything. But remember to fill me in if she did. I don't need the sofa sleuths keeping secrets from me."

I half smiled when he mentioned how

Beth and I occasionally referred to ourselves. "Right. Then I'll head over to the hospital and check on Fiona."

"I can drive you if you'd like."

"That's okay. If they release her, I'll bring her back to my place for the night."

"Good. That will give us time to finish our investigation of the store and apartment."

I snapped my fingers. "Dang, what about the black dust you're about to flick everywhere?"

His lips thinned. "Right."

"Do you ever get tired of saying, *right*?"

"I choose the word that fits the current situation, and I don't want Fiona to worry about cleaning her apartment once she leaves the hospital."

"If you give me the 'all clear' I'll take care of it." I used air quotes around *all clear* to indicate that I understood it wouldn't be until after they had gathered every bit of pertinent evidence.

"Excellent." He grinned. "See what I did there?"

At least this time he hadn't used the word *right* again. I shook my head but smiled. "You're incorrigible."

His eyes were somber. "Gigi, I'm sorry you got pulled into another difficult situation."

I melted a bit when he called me by the nickname he had given me. It was sweet and showed a different side of his cop persona, which I found pretty attractive.

"It's no one's fault. I'm glad Fiona and I had dinner plans, so it was discovered she needed help. I shudder to think she could have lain on the floor all night." I didn't say it, but I wondered if she could have died if she had been alone and bleeding all night.

"You found her." He slipped an arm around my shoulders. "I'm confident she'll make a full recovery."

"We should go inside." I pulled away from his half embrace. He was my best friend's cousin, and I had a business to build. I couldn't allow any burgeoning feelings to surface.

"Right." He grinned. "See what I did there?"

"Eddie." I laughed. "Thanks for being you." I had a feeling the word, right, was about to become a running joke between us. I walked to the street side of the alley, anxious to get away from the shadow-filled space. I kept my eyes on the ground when I stopped. "Do you have an evidence bag?"

"What did you find?" He knelt next to me.

"A cupcake wrapper. And look—it's not dried out. I'll bet the intruder ate the cupcake and then littered. If nothing else, you can arrest him for that."

He picked up the wrapper with the evidence bag turned inside out and sealed it. "Good eyes."

We walked the rest of the alley without finding anything else. Once on the sidewalk, I looked around. "He could have gone anywhere. If he were a local, he would have blended right in."

"That's true, but either way, we'll find him. By the 'we'll,' I mean the police force, not the sofa sleuths."

"It doesn't matter what you say. I'll keep my eyes open and my brain engaged in figuring this out."

"You're building your dress design business. From what Beth has said, it's going well. You have several brides you're working with and a steady clientele for off-the-rack items."

I gave him a sharp look. "You asked about what's happening in my little shop?"

"Gigi, I want you to be a smashing success so that you'll stay in town. Someday…"

Rhonda came out of Twice Loved. "Eddie, did you find anything?"

Uncertain whether to feel relieved by the interruption or disappointed, I walked away from Eddie and headed inside to find Beth. I noticed the blood on the floor and made a mental note to ask about when I could clean it up. Then, there was the other concern about how to remove it without leaving a stain. That was something I could look up online.

"Claudia, over here." Beth waved to me from the back of the store, where the area rugs were on display.

I wound my way around tables and furniture down a long aisle until I reached the room. "What did you find?"

"First, tell me what you and Eddie discovered. You were gone for quite a while, and Rhonda seemed annoyed the entire time. She kept huffing and grumbling. I couldn't hear what she was saying, but she didn't seem pleased."

"Factoid. The intruder was still in the building when I arrived."

Her eyes grew wide. "How do you know that?"

"It's going to sound peculiar, but he took a cupcake from the box."

She jerked her head back. "What?"

"And we found the wrapper in the alley between the inn and the store. Eddie thinks that's how he got away unnoticed."

"That's bizarre. Anything else?"

"He went through Fiona's desk, but the rest of the apartment was untouched. Either he didn't have time, or he knew where to look for whatever he wanted."

"Money had to be the motive."

"Have you found anything of interest?"

She shook her head. "Not a thing. Everything seems to be orderly. Fiona can tell instantly if anything was disturbed; she'll know what should have been on that table. Then we can tell Eddie what's been stolen and add it to the report."

"I'm going to take a picture and show it to her when I get to the hospital."

She slipped her arm through mine. "When *we* get to the hospital. You've had a shock today, reminding you of your Uncle Herman's unfortunate circumstances."

I dipped my chin. "At least Fiona didn't

become a ghost." Not that Beth knew Herman's ghost was still hanging around my dress shop, and that was something I wouldn't share.

She grasped my hand. "Let's tell Eddie we're going to the hospital."

Nodding, I let her lead me to the front. I paused to take a few more pictures of the now-empty table.

He came over to us and gestured to the floor. "I'll take care of this and meet you at the hospital. If Fiona's released before I arrive, do you still plan on taking her to your place, Claudia?"

"Yes, I don't want her to be alone tonight. But tomorrow, we'll get her apartment and store back in order, if that's okay."

Eddie nodded. "It should be fine."

"Great. We'll be on our way to the hospital, then."

Beth said, "And I'm going with her."

Rhonda came up to us. "Where are you going?"

The icy stare made the hair on the back of my neck stand on end. This new addition to the police force was hostile. "To the hospital. Any objections?"

Her brow arched, and she smirked. "Officer Jacobs, have you questioned this witness? She might be the attacker."

"You've got to be kidding," I exclaimed, slapping my hand against my forehead. "Why is it that every cop I meet places me at the top of their suspect list?"

4

———

*E*ddie said, "Claudia Grant did not attack Fiona Doyle."

Rhonda asked, "How can you be sure?"

I watched as the officers sparred.

"Claudia is a good family friend and very close to Ms. Doyle. I'll stake my reputation on Claudia's character any day."

Beth said, "I agree. You're chasing the wrong suspect, Officer Perkins."

Her face flushed pink when Beth spoke up. "And you are?"

She locked eyes with the officer. "Beth

Stewart. You might have heard of my father, Ethan Stewart, who is also a close, personal friend of Claudia's."

"The former chief is your father?"

"And my uncle," Eddie said. "Now, the ladies will be on their way to the hospital." He glanced at me. "Please text with an update on Fiona's condition."

"Sure. What can I tell her? You know she'll ask."

"It's an active investigation, and we'll catch whoever broke in. But for now, don't tell her about the cupcake. She'll worry about you getting caught in the crossfire, and if I know Fiona, she'll refuse to stay with you out of a misplaced sense of protecting you."

Rhonda tilted her head. "Cupcake?"

Eddie ignored her, and I nodded. "Can I tell her you said you'd give her an update when you've completed surveying the scene?"

"Yes."

"I left my shoulder bag upstairs. Is it ok if I take it and Fiona's too?"

"I'll get them. You stay here."

Before I could protest, he jogged through the store and up the stairs.

Rhonda said, "What's this about a cupcake?"

I glanced over my shoulder, wishing Eddie would magically appear. "I brought a box of four cupcakes from Brewed Bliss and a pint of ice cream for dessert. When Eddie and I went upstairs I noticed only three, and we found a discarded cupcake wrapper in the alley."

She stared at me. "Is that all?"

"Yes. Eddie has the wrapper in an evidence bag."

"What makes you think it was from your cupcake purchase?"

I didn't appreciate the hostility in her tone. Deciding not to antagonize her further, I said, "You know how when a cupcake liner gets crinkled and dried out after it's left on the table? This one was still moist. It might be a leap to think it was from my box, but it had chocolate cake crumbs and pink icing smeared, just like what I bought. Besides, I don't believe in coincidence. Do you?"

Eddie walked over to us. "Here you go." He handed me my bag along with a black handbag. "This was the only one I found, and Fiona's wallet is inside, along with her key ring."

"Thanks." I gave him a tight smile. "Beth, I'm going to stop at my place. I'll pick you up in about ten minutes?"

"I'll drive. It might be tough for Fiona to get into your Jeep. My SUV isn't as high."

Eddie's fingertips grazed my hand. "Text me after you see Fiona?"

His gentle blue-gray eyes calmed my frayed nerves. "You bet."

Beth and I exited the front door onto Main Street.

"Could you give me ten minutes?"

She said, "Sure. I'll be out front. Take your time."

She crossed the intersection of Main and Cade Street, and I hurried to my shop. I entered through the front door.

"Herman?" I strode through the salon and into the workroom. "I need to talk to you."

Lola dashed down the stairs and ribboned around my ankles. "Hello, little girl. Where is your favorite ghost?"

She meowed, which was zero help. I picked her up and dashed up the stairs. "Herman?" This time, my voice held a sharp tone. I had little time to wait for him to make a dramatic entrance.

His ghostly form reclined on the sofa. "Yes, my girl? How can I help you? Wait, aren't you supposed to be having dinner with Fiona?"

I placed Lola next to him, who promptly curled into a comma shape.

"Yes, but what do you know about her inventory?"

He moved to a perched position on the arm of the sofa. "Ask her."

"She was attacked earlier and is in the hospital. Eddie and another police officer are currently investigating, but would she have items that are so valuable someone might be willing to harm her?"

"Is she going to be all right?"

"When the EMTs took her, she was lucid and talking. She might need stitches in the back of her head, but head wounds bleed a lot, so maybe not. It will depend on how deep the gash was."

Herman's ghostly form now slid in front of the living room windows as if he were pacing. "She has some antiques, mostly furniture, the occasional rare necklace or pocket watch, but nothing priceless. Twice Loved is about trinkets and the customers who appreciate quality, well-crafted older furniture."

That had been my impression, too.

"What does Eddie think happened?"

"A burglary, and Fiona interrupted them. There is one upsetting thing."

He floated to me. "What?"

"Whoever it was that attacked her was in the apartment when I arrived. Of course, I didn't know it at the time. I placed the dessert I brought on the small bench beside the back door before rushing downstairs to help her. When I returned upstairs with Eddie, we discovered a missing cupcake, and the wrapper was tossed in the alley."

"That's interesting." He stroked his chin, a gesture I surmised he had made while living.

"Does Fiona have any enemies?"

"You've met her. What do you think?"

I shook my head. "I didn't think so, but since you were close when you were alive, I thought you might know something that could help."

"I can't think of a single time when anyone was cross with her. She treats all customers like friends; if they were looking for something specific, she'd do her best to find it."

"You mean like finding the right table or wall print?"

"Yes. Like she found that rug you have in your bedroom. She knew how I had decorated it and, on a hunch, found the perfect rug in case you wanted one."

"Fiona's very thoughtful." I crossed to the windows and saw Beth pulling out of her parking lot. "I need to run. Beth's driving me to the hospital. If Fiona's discharged, I'm going to bring her home with me tonight."

"You're a good person, Claudia. Returning to her place tonight might be unnerving."

"Exactly. Keep an eye on our place. The intruder probably knows I was there."

"Lock up, and don't worry; if anyone breaks in here, I'll see if I can work up a scare or two and send them packing."

Laughing softly, I said, "Oh, Herman,

there are times I wish I could hug the stuffing out of you."

"Knowing you'd like to is enough." He called after me, "Turn the security cameras on."

Uncertain how long we would be at the hospital, I filled Lola's bowls with kitty kibble and fresh water. I raised a hand in acknowledgment, closed the apartment door to the shop, and locked the deadbolt before exiting through the back door. If someone tried to break into the store, they would have difficulty getting into my apartment.

Beth waved as I reached the vehicle. "Is everything okay?"

I buckled up. "Yes, I wanted to check on Lola and feed her in case we get home late."

She grinned. "Lola's a cute but demanding little fluff ball."

"Did you call your dad and let him know what's happened?"

She eased onto the road. "Yes. He's going

to the store to see if he can help. I suggested the blood spot on the floor."

"That's a great idea. Eddie mentioned he would take care of it, but he's quite busy with Officer Rhonda Perkins."

"Yeah, that's one girl who instantly disliked us." Clicking on her blinker, Beth turned off Cade Street and picked up speed as we headed west.

"Any idea what her deal is?"

"Other than the fact that she's new in town, I have no idea. We should discuss the case before we see Fiona."

I withdrew my cell and began to scroll through the pictures I had taken. "Eddie told me the sofa sleuths should stay out of the investigation."

With a laugh, Beth said, "Right. In six months, this is our first opportunity to flex our brain power to help thwart a bad guy."

"Somehow, he thinks our enthusiasm is misplaced. But I'm excited, too." I elaborated on the first picture of the space table. "There's an outline of a rectangle. I'm guessing it's about the width of a shoebox."

"Or a book?"

I scrolled to the next picture. "A few leather-bound books and a small stack of linen napkins are stacked at the back of the table. It seems like a box of something was moved. Did you notice anything out of place?"

"Not a single speck of dust. It appeared that Fiona had merely walked around the room and tidied everything up."

"What if," my eyes widened, "she was in the store tidying up and came across the table. Someone snuck up behind her and conked her on the head."

"She does like the store to be ready to open on Monday morning, and she said she thought it was around four when she heard something."

Beth smacked the steering wheel. "What if she went down and the person was already in the store, waiting to get out unnoticed? In-

stead of exiting through the back, they pan-
icked and hit her to buy time to escape."

"Then why go upstairs and toss her desk? She must have had something they wanted."

"Or it was a distraction."

Turning in the passenger seat, I said, "So they found what they wanted, heard me come in, hid until I went upstairs for my phone, then took the cupcake and snuck out?"

"Sure. Taking the box with them. So, once we know what was in the box, we can figure out who would have wanted it."

"Easy peasy." A sign for the emergency room was up ahead. "We'll get our answers soon enough."

Beth parked the car close to the automatic glass doors. I slipped my phone into my bag and took Fiona's purse. We entered the waiting room. A couple of people were sitting in uncomfortable-looking plastic chairs with vacant stares at a news program on the wall-mounted television.

We approached the desk clerk. "Hello, I'm Claudia Grant, and this is Beth Stewart. We're friends of Fiona Doyle. She was brought in with a head injury."

He tapped the keys without looking up and scanned the screen. "Ms. Doyle's with the doctor. I'll let someone know you're here. You can take a seat over there." He bobbed his head toward the waiting area.

"Thank you." I followed Beth to a section of empty chairs.

"Not very chatty." I glanced at the desk clerk.

"I think they keep the distant demeanor so they're not asked questions they can't answer."

"True." I held Fiona's bag in my lap. I hadn't spent any time in a hospital waiting room and wasn't sure what we were supposed to do.

"Did you have any luck with the notion books?"

I gave her a quizzical smile. "Huh?"

"The buttons you need for the bridal gown."

A sigh escaped me. "No. I was hoping to find something perfect at Fiona's today. But that's on the back burner. Hopefully, Mrs. Vanderkemp won't be on the phone early tomorrow morning expecting an update."

"Don't hold your breath. From how you've described her, she sounds like she'll be one of those mothers of the bride who will hound everyone involved in the wedding over every detail."

"Thank goodness her husband was a sweetheart. He popped in during the fitting and said that whatever his daughter wanted, she should have. Of course, Mrs. V rolled her eyes while Betsy, her best friend, beamed as if it were normal for Mr. Vanderkemp to indulge his daughter."

"No one from the groom's family was there to witness the transformation from fiancée to bride?"

"From what I gathered, the groom's

mother has passed away, but his sister was there and somewhat supportive. The ladies didn't seem close, as if Sienna attended out of obligation rather than genuine interest. Of course, she's happy that I'm designing her dress. In an interesting twist, the future husband popped his head into the store. When Julia saw him, she barred him from entering, saying he wasn't getting any preview of coming attractions."

"I bet that must have been uncomfortable."

"Not at all. Tristan was having a good time teasing his bride. He and Mr. Vanderkemp were going someplace together. I wonder if he and Sienna are twins. They have similar builds and facial structure."

"Brothers and sisters often do."

Buttons and bridal gowns were the last things I wanted to occupy my mind. I shifted in the hard chair. "You'd think these chairs would have some cushioning, considering how long some people have to wait."

"It probably has more to do with ease of disinfecting than comfort."

A man dressed in deep blue scrubs and a white coat hurried into the waiting room. "Family of Ms. Doyle?"

Beth and I got to our feet.

He pointed to the door he had come out of. "Follow me."

We hurried after him.

"How's Fiona?" I asked.

"Let's wait until we get inside."

We entered an examination area. The white privacy curtain raced over the rod with a flick of his wrist. "Fiona, your family is here."

She opened her eyes and smiled at us. "Girls. I'm happy to see you both."

"Ms. Doyle, is it okay for me to provide an update with the ladies here?"

She nodded. "Yes, they're the closest I have to family."

Beth went on one side of the bed, and I went on the other. She looked frail in the hospital bed against the crisp white linens with an IV dripping into her arm. I took her hand.

He stuck his hands in his lab coat pockets. "She's going to be fine. We scanned her head, and there was no internal bleeding. She'll need a couple of stitches, but she's one tough lady. We plan on keeping her overnight for observation. She lost a lot of blood."

"Thank you, Doctor. This is good news."

He stepped out of the room.

Squeezing my hand, she said, "Tell me everything that's happening at my store. Have the police caught the intruder yet?"

"I'm afraid not yet, Fiona. Eddie Jacobs and a new officer are at the store, and Ethan is going over."

"He's one of the good guys and knows how to get the job done."

"Fiona, Dad's not a police officer any longer."

"I know, but he has a sharp eye and mind. With his experience, he might see something the younger police officers could overlook."

There was logic I couldn't argue with. "Eddie said he'd be along to talk with you later."

She closed her eyes. "You heard the doc. They want to keep me here for the night. Observation, they say."

"That's okay. Do you want us to get you something from your apartment?" I glanced at Beth, who nodded.

"We'd be happy to run home for you."

"Not tonight, but I'll need fresh clothes tomorrow if you don't mind. I'll have to throw out the blouse I'm wearing."

Beth said, "We're happy to help."

"Thank you. Now tell me, why do you think someone was skulking around my store?"

I withdrew my cell and looked over my shoulder to ask her a couple of questions before we got interrupted. "I took a few pictures near where I found you." Tapping the screen, I pulled up the picture. "Is this table missing something?"

Fiona took my cell. "Do you have more pictures?"

"Yes, scroll to the right."

Thumbing through the pictures, her frown deepened. "Were there other open spaces on bookcases or display areas?"

I shook my head. "No. Just this one. Does it mean something?"

Handing my phone back to me, she closed her eyes. A lone tear trickled from the corner and absorbed into the pillow.

"Fiona, what is it?"

"I can't believe I've become a statistic of violence in a bucolic town like Drakes Bay."

"It's very distressing. Was there something taken from the table?" I had to know what she was holding back.

"It's insignificant compared to the treasures in the shop," she said, looking me in the eye. "I'm sorry, Claudia. I found the buttons you needed for the gown you're redesigning, but the box has been stolen."

5

I blinked rapidly as I tried to process the idea that someone would steal a box of old buttons. Their value might be a mere twenty dollars. They're not worth breaking into a store and injuring an older woman.

"Are you certain the box wasn't there?"

She winced as she nodded. "I found them in the back room. I intended to take them up to my apartment to show you during dinner. While dusting, I set them down to finish organizing things. You know

I like a tidy shop. When I noticed the back door ajar, I called out for you, Claudia, thinking you'd arrived early. The next thing I remember is you rubbing my hand, telling me to open my eyes."

Beth asked, "Was the box something you had just acquired?"

"Yes. It was a find from an estate sale. It's from down east. I purchased it from one of those estate auction websites online."

"Is that something you do regularly?"

"Oh, yes. It's a fantastic way to uncover amazing deals. I've always been lucky to find treasures long forgotten. People constantly tuck things into a box, never looking at them again." Her brows knitted together. "But why take a box of fancy buttons?"

I glanced at Beth before responding. "It must have contained something important. We should check the auction site to see if we can find any connections to the original owners beyond that one box."

"I purchased four at that auction. They are

marked with the company name Bucks and Bidding Auction Services."

"Have you opened them?"

"Not yet." Her eyes widened. "Did someone go through the other boxes while I was unconscious?"

"Eddie didn't mention that any boxes had been opened in your back room." I didn't want to add more stress to the poor woman. "However, this could be an important clue. They went through your desk in your apartment."

She shut her eyes. "I'm not surprised. They'd want to know what else I bought at the auction."

"Do you happen to know other shop owners who purchased items from that auction?"

"No, it would involve people from all over the country—and perhaps even the globe—virtually shopping at these online events. Everything is shipped within three days of the auction. Think of them as being similar to a fancy art auction, but much less expensive."

I understood what she meant, it would be like finding a needle in a pin box. "When did you purchase the items?"

"Two, no, three weeks ago, I saw the buttons advertised and bought them for you. Occasionally, I would find lace and other accoutrements for Herman at auctions."

I pressed a hand over my heart. "That's so nice of you. I'm sorry it's led to your attack."

She waved a hand. "I'm a tough one. It'll take more than a knock on the head to slow me down." Pulling the blanket up a little higher, she closed her eyes. "I've got a nasty headache, and these bright overhead lights aren't helping."

"What did they give you for the pain?" Beth took her hand and sat down.

"Nothing yet. They have to make sure the scan's clear first."

The results were ready, and she needed pain medication. "I'll be right back."

I bobbed my head to the nurse's desk, and Beth said, "I'll stay here."

I crossed the room. "Excuse me."

A woman looked up and smiled. "Yes?"

"Mrs. Doyle is complaining of a headache and mentioned that she can't have anything until her scan results are back, but the doctor in dark blue scrubs said they were available and that she was fine; she's just being kept for observation."

"We're waiting on transport to the floor."

"Can she get something for the pain?" I didn't want to state the obvious, but she needed something to ease the discomfort.

"Let me check her chart, and I'll be over in a moment."

"Thank you," I said as I walked back to Fiona. I paused and took a deep breath. With a smile on my face, I added, "Good news! The nurse will give you some medication, and then the transport team will be along to take you to your room."

"Claudia, you and Beth are such sweet girls."

"You'd do the same for us." I sat on the edge of the bed.

"Since Herman died, I've been out of sorts. I lost my best friend."

How should I respond to that statement? From conversations with a ghost, I knew he loved her dearly and regretted that they hadn't spent more time together. "You inherited me. I know it's not the same as having Herman, but…"

She pushed herself up to her elbow. "That's one way to look at it. And the best way."

The nurse bustled in. "Ms. Doyle, I have some pain medication." She pushed a button, and the bed adjusted to a seated position. Handing her a cup with a straw and a smaller plastic cup containing two pills, she said, "You should feel better soon."

Fiona popped them into her mouth and took a sip of water. "Thank you."

The nurse caught my eye. "If she needs something else, just let me know."

"I will." I turned my attention to Fiona, wondering if she remembered anything else about the auction. But she had closed her eyes; there was time to sort that out later.

Beth and I sat quietly. My mind raced with possibilities. Who ran the auction site? Did they keep a list of contents in a box they sold? Would they have the names or contact information of anyone else who might have bid on it?

A deep voice pulled me from my thoughts. Eddie. "I'm looking for Mrs. Doyle."

I lifted my hand in a small wave.

"Ms. Doyle," the nurse said as she pushed back the curtain, revealing Eddie standing behind her. "There's an officer here. Are you feeling up to his visit?"

Fiona opened her eyes. "Officer Eddie. Do you have good news?"

"I'm sorry, Fiona, we don't know who

broke in yet, but we're actively pursuing all leads. Would you mind answering a few questions?"

"I've told Claudia and Beth all I know."

He kept his gaze focused on her. "Would you mind going over it again?"

If he were annoyed with us, it wouldn't show.

"The girls showed me the pictures they took of my store. I bought a box from an on-line auction a couple of weeks ago that's now missing. I spent around twenty dollars plus shipping. Nothing spectacular. If they had been that important to someone, I would have gladly given them the darn box. Claudia can fill you in on the details, and the rifling through my desk? I'm sure they were looking for information on the transaction." She cocked a brow. "Unless you saw other boxes ripped open in my storage area?"

"No, ma'am. But I will have police presence there during the night for an extra measure of protection." He jotted down a few notes. "You have no idea who might have known about the box?"

She pursed her lips. "No, I unpacked it earlier today and planned to give it to Claudia. She's been searching for antique buttons for a dress she's redesigning."

"Are you sure there were buttons in the box?"

Her eyes narrowed. "Detective Eddie, it was an antique cigar box filled with mismatched buttons and miscellaneous trinkets."

He glanced my way. "Did you tell anyone about this?"

"The bride and her family know I'm sourcing replacement buttons for her wedding gown, and I mentioned them to Beth."

"I didn't have anything suitable, so I gave Claudia a few catalogs to look through."

He tapped the pen to the pad. "Is there anything you can think of—any detail—no matter how small, about earlier today? Did you hear any sounds? Get a funny feeling like you were being watched? Smell cologne or perfume?"

"No, other than when I heard someone. I thought Claudia had arrived early and called out to her."

"Because you were having dinner. That makes sense. And nothing like this has ever happened before?"

"Oh, my heavens. Never." She placed a hand over her heart. "My little business doesn't attract much attention, except from shoppers on a rainy day. I've been in business for over thirty-five years. There have been occasional shoplifters, but usually it's bored kids trying to see if they can get one over on me."

He tapped the bedcovers. "Thank you, Fiona. I'll be in touch if I have more questions."

She grabbed his hand. "What about my store and apartment? Will it be safe to return?"

"I believe this was an isolated incident.

The intruder took what they sought and won't return. Additionally, Ethan and I will repair the locks to ensure your safety. You might want to consider installing front and back door cameras for added security."

Frowning, she said, "No. I won't let this change how I live."

"All right. If you change your mind, I can recommend some companies."

"Thank you."

A woman in lavender scrubs appeared. "Ms. Doyle. I'm here to take you upstairs."

"Okay," she said. "Claudia, you and Beth run along. I'm going to sleep off this headache. I'd be very grateful if you could bring me fresh clothes in the morning and drive me home."

"Of course. I'll call you tomorrow." I kissed her cheek. "Rest."

We stepped away from her bed as the aide eased it into the hallway. We made an interesting trio as we left the emergency room, which was quiet for now.

Once the doors closed behind us, I scanned the parking lot. We were alone. "Did you learn anything new at Fiona's?"

"No. The lock on the back door was picked, but it wasn't broken, just like upstairs. Nothing damaged, just a mess, and I'm sure the perp wore gloves or wiped down surfaces."

"Not even the cupcake box?"

He shook his head. "Just yours. I'm assuming Sue wore gloves when she packed it?"

"Yes, what about the store floor?"

"Clean as white cotton."

The fabric reference was something I liked. "What do you mean just mine? Do you have my fingerprints?"

"Yes, from when Colton Prescott was murdered."

My shoulders slumped. "Now I feel like a criminal."

He rubbed my shoulder. "If it makes you feel better, we have Beth's, too."

She laughed. "The sofa sleuths made it into the database? Cool." She clapped him on the back. "Will we be able to get into Fiona's in the morning, tidy the place up, and get her clean clothes?"

"The scene will be released by then. If not, I'll go over there with you."

He nodded toward Beth's SUV as he strode to the police sedan. "Drive carefully, ladies."

I waited until he got into the vehicle and drove away. "Beth, don't you find it interesting that this is the first time Fiona's ever had a problem at her store?"

"And it comes on the heels of her buying something from an auction?"

"The positive is they didn't want to hurt Fiona." I gave her a pointed look. "Are you thinking what I'm thinking?"

She grinned. "We're going to your place to warm the markers up?"

"Exactly. This item was targeted, and we will find out the why and who. Besides, you heard what Eddie said—they've chalked this up as a one-off. A box of buttons is of zero value."

"What if there were gems in that box of discarded buttons?"

I liked Beth's direction. "We need to return to my place and jot down these ideas. Can we stop for a pizza on the way?"

"Is this Maine?" she laughed.

*B*ack at my place, the first thing I did was set up the whiteboard. Now, I had plates, forks, and napkins on the table. Beth was getting the glasses. Herman hovered around the kitchen, wanting to know everything about Fiona. I was trying to figure out how to organize my scattered thoughts to recap the events for my friendly ghost.

I put slices of pizza and the salad, which Beth thought was a good idea, on our plates.

"We should review everything that happened to get a complete picture."

Holding the glasses, she said, "Do you want to be the scribe?"

"Sure. Keep Lola away from my dinner." The fur ball circled my legs as I shuffled into the living room. "She has an affinity to human food."

Beth laughed. "Lola, hop up on the sofa and get comfy while two of your favorite humans get their brains in gear."

Lola flicked her tail.

Herman floated beside me, his eyes locked on my plate. "I miss pizza."

I picked up a bright purple marker and wrote a list in the middle.

Cigar box with buttons, online auction value: $20

Fiona

Desk trashed

Other boxes untouched

Locks picked

4:00

Perp hung around

Beth waved her fork. "Don't forget the stolen cupcake."

I jotted it down. "Now," I took a bite of pizza. "This is what we know. What don't we know?"

"The who and why."

"They knew the shop was closed, but they didn't know about Fiona's habit of tidying up, which suggests they weren't local. Is that possible?"

"Sure, if they had been tracking the box since the auction. Since it had been in their family before the sale, they wanted it, and when they discovered it had been sold, they traced it here."

"Why not simply ask Fiona for it and purchase it?"

Beth crunched on a cucumber slice dripping with ranch dressing. "Whatever was in the box was valuable, and they were afraid Fiona wouldn't give it to them?"

I liked that she answered my question on her own. "Hypothetically speaking, if a family heirloom in the box were priceless, some unethical people wouldn't have returned it. They might have said they purchased it fairly and expected to be compensated."

"You believe there was something valuable in the box, and rather than asking Fiona, they chose to steal it."

"I do, and they must be searching for more items, so they searched her papers for something else. We'll contact Bucks and Bidding Auction Services tomorrow to see what we can uncover. If we're wrong, there's no harm; but if we're right and more is happening here, we'll turn the information over to Eddie."

Herman's transparent form whizzed around me. "If you want my input, I'm betting whoever it is has visited or lives in our charming town."

Unable to ask him why, I echoed his statement to Beth.

She nodded. "I think you're right. Who-ever attacked Fiona is still here."

As I sank into the chair, Herman's ghostly hand looked like he was trying to pat my shoulder. "This wasn't something straightfor-ward. There's much more to the story." I tapped my midsection. "I got that floppy flip-ping again."

6

$\mathcal{I}$ woke more convinced that this burglary wasn't as straightforward as Eddie might think. I had already received a call from Fiona stating she would be released midmorning. She was particular about what she wanted me to bring for clothes and a hat to cover her stitches. I failed to mention that Beth and I were going to do a little investigating before picking her up, and were meeting at Twice Loved at seven thirty.

Herman hovered in my bedroom

doorway as I made the bed. "Good morning. Any news on Fiona?"

"She called a few minutes ago. Beth and I'll pick her up in a couple of hours. But first, we'll poke around the shop and apartment."

"Do you hope to find evidence of who might have hurt Fiona?"

"That's my plan. It's just a guess, but I think that person has been tracking the shipment from the auction and knew exactly what they were looking for. If Fiona hadn't unpacked it to show me, they would have gone through the other boxes in the storage room."

"I guess they'd know which ones came from that auction based on the boxes labeled with Bucks and Bidding."

"Exactly. I'll take a picture of the cartons and contact the auctioneer to see if I can track down where the items originated. Then we should have a trail to follow."

I crossed the room, and Herman floated

down the hall ahead of me. "Be careful today."

"Thanks, but don't worry. Eddie said the police would monitor the store last night and the scene has been released. If we see anything out of the ordinary when we arrive, we'll call Eddie or Ethan."

He leaned against the counter. I fixed Lola's breakfast, and the sound of the can top popping lured her around the corner from the entrance hall.

Meow.

"Well, good morning, little miss." I filled her food and water bowls and set them on the small mat near her. "Now, coffee and a quick breakfast before I'm off."

"Do you think tracking down where the items came from is safe?"

"Herman, I understand your concern, but let's consider it another way. What if the box that was taken didn't contain what the burglar wanted, and they make a return trip after Fiona comes home from the hospital? She's already in a weakened state from her injury. The best thing we can do is to track down the information."

He shook his finger at me. "You should let the police do that. They're trained professionals."

I arched a brow and drummed the counter with my fingers. "The professionals seem to think this was a random theft. They aren't going to inquire any deeper." I held up my hand. "Before you ask how I know, Eddie said as much last night as we were leaving the hospital."

"Does Beth agree with you?"

"You were there last night when we were reviewing the clues."

His ghostly shoulders slumped. "I'm in two camps. I'm happy you want to help Fiona, but the other side of the coin is putting yourself in danger."

"No one is going to give a dress designer another thought. I've already decided what to say when I contact the auction house."

"Have you?"

"I'm searching for antique buttons and lace for my design business, and Fiona Doyle's recent purchase was stunning. Is there any chance I could find out which estate sale they were from so I could contact the person handling the estate to see if more items will be listed for auction?" A smile curved my lips. "Pretty clever, don't you agree?"

"What if they say there aren't any more from that particular client?"

"Don't burst my sleuth bubble. I'll figure that out if I need a backup plan." I poured coffee into a travel cup, scarfed down a banana, and grabbed a sunshine muffin from the bakery box on the counter. "See you later."

I didn't want to cause my resident ghost any concern about me poking my nose where it might not belong. What Herman didn't know couldn't upset him.

I skipped down the back steps, crossed in

front of the Whistlers Inn, and circled through the alley to discover Beth was sitting on the front stoop of Twice Loved.

"Morning," she called out as she rubbed her hands together. "How did you sleep?"

"Not great. You?"

"Me neither. I still can't believe someone would break into Fiona's place and assault her for a cigar box."

"It's awful." I casually looked around as I grew closer, hoping no one was within hearing distance. A few people were strolling to the beach access, but otherwise, it was just us. "When I spoke with Fiona, she told me where she had hidden a key to the apartment."

"I thought she might."

We wandered to the back of the shop and enjoyed the view before circling the building. I lowered my voice. "Do you think we look casual?"

She laughed. "Those people aren't paying

attention to us at all. The ocean view has completely captivated them."

I deposited the muffin wrapper in a trash bin on the sidewalk and handed Beth my coffee. "There's a combination to the box," explaining why I needed her to hold my drink.

I knelt on the ground before a flower bed, lifted the red paver closest to the door, and found the box underneath, just as Fiona had described it: a slim, black security case with a tumbler lock.

I replaced the paver and turned the dials. It sprang open effortlessly, but it was empty inside. "There can't be more than one box planted under the paver."

Beth leaned in. "I wouldn't think so. What are we going to do?"

I replaced it, shifting things around to make it seem like it hadn't been disturbed. "Should we call Eddie?"

A frown graced her lips. "He's not going to be happy we're here."

"That's only if he knows we're looking for

clues. We have a valid reason to be here—gathering clothes for Fiona's release."

With a laugh, she remarked, "I love the creative ways you spin events."

I glanced up the stairs. "The excuse of clothes might work if it weren't so early and we weren't together." I nodded. "I'm going to try the door." The window was also an option if, by some slim chance, Eddie had forgotten to lock it, and the screen was still off.

"Come on." I crept up the steps with Beth following behind me. I glanced over my shoulder when we reached the deck and scanned the area, but still no one was paying attention to us. Nevertheless, I couldn't shake the feeling that we were being watched. I attributed it to nerves after what had happened yesterday afternoon.

At first, I saw that the screen was in place, blocking that access point. I lifted the doormat, hoping we might find a key or one hidden beneath the potted plants. Nothing. Beth stepped around me.

"Any new ideas?"

Beth grabbed my arm. "The door is ajar."

"Well, that was an obvious miss on my part."

"Claudia, I only saw it because you were dealing with the logical hiding places for a key."

"Should we call Eddie?" I craned my neck to look from left to right through the glass. "I don't see anyone. "

"Let's take a moment and think about the possibilities."

I nodded. "It could be just a mistake, like whoever pulled the door closed didn't notice it wasn't latched, and the wind eased it open during the night."

"Or someone else knew where the key was, which is why it wasn't in the box when you opened it, and let themselves in to poke around."

"The other possibility is that someone returned for another look after being interrupted the first time. In this case, we should go inside and try to catch them in the act. Then we can call Eddie."

"Bold. I like the last option."

With a grin, I took my coffee mug from Beth and placed it near the door. "You can change your mind."

Her eyes twinkled with mischief. "Are you kidding? This is going to be the highlight of my day."

I laughed. "Mine, too."

Using my finger, I nudged the door open wider, hoping the hinges were well oiled. Once it was fully open, I stepped inside and paused, listening for any sounds that indicated someone was there. But it was silent as a tomb.

"Ready? I whispered.

She nodded.

I entered the apartment, and it appeared untouched from what I could see in the living room directly ahead of us. I turned to the right, into the laundry room and kitchen, where everything was tidy as well. Beth pointed down the hall toward the bedroom and office areas. We both knew the layout intimately since our apartments were essentially the same. We crept slowly down the hall, doing our best to keep our footsteps quiet. I grabbed an umbrella from the hallway and slipped ahead of Beth. If anyone popped out, I could clobber them.

A rustling sound came from Fiona's room. I raised my hand to stop Beth from entering. Pointing to her phone, I mouthed, *"Text Eddie."* She nodded, and I waited while she sent the message. Giving me a thumbs-up, I held up three fingers. One by one, I folded them into my palm. On three, I pushed open the door, and with the umbrella raised high, I shouted, "Freeze!"

Rhonda Perkins whirled around. "What are you doing here?"

I kept the umbrella over my head. "We could ask you the same question."

"Investigating."

Beth asked, "Out of uniform?"

"The clothes don't matter when you're on the job." She placed a stack of envelopes on top of the dresser.

I thrust my chin up. "They do if you entered the building without the shop owner's permission."

Her eyes narrowed. "I could say the same about you. Only you're entering an active crime scene."

"Are not." That sounded childish. "Fiona asked us to get her clothes and a hat. She's being released today."

"And you're bringing her back here?"

"Why wouldn't we? This is her home." Beth stood firmly beside me.

Her eyes darted to the door. "It's an active crime scene."

"Not from what Eddie said when we saw him at the hospital. This was just an unfortunate break-in where someone was assaulted, and the perp got away."

Rhonda shifted from one foot to the other.

In my mind, that was an indicator that she was guilty of something.

"How did you get in?"

"I found a key under the doormat. I'm surprised people still do that."

"Residents in small towns typically are trusting."

"Are you from a small town, Claudia?"

"Actually, I moved here from New York City, and before that, Boston." I wasn't about to let the police officer change the subject.

Footsteps thumped up the back stairs, and I heard Eddie say, "Beth? Claudia? What's going on in here?"

"He's not much on stealth, is he?"

"In the text, I said we found Rhonda in the apartment."

And he wouldn't think there was anything amiss with a cop at the scene. Was this déjà vu?

He was behind us. "Rhonda, what are you doing here? We cleared the scene last night."

She flushed a deep shade of red as he looked her over from head to toe.

"If you're here on official business, why aren't you in uniform?"

"That's what we want to know," Beth exclaimed.

"Ladies, would you go into the living room?"

I shook my head. "Sorry. We have permission to be here. She doesn't."

With her hands on her hips, she said, "I do, as an officer of the Drakes Bay Police Department."

Eddie, wearing his police uniform, said, "Rhonda, we should step outside and talk. The ladies are here to pick up a few things for Fiona."

Before she left, she reached for the stack of envelopes but drew her hand back before taking them. Just as I suspected, she wasn't here in an official capacity; otherwise, she wouldn't have hesitated.

Rhonda walked in front of Beth and me, pushing past Eddie before continuing down the hall. I looked at her feet and saw that she was wearing sneakers. Then I noticed the outline of her gun visible at the waistband of her jeans under her top. When I pointed it out to Beth, her eyes widened.

I waited for the screen door to bang, pulled Beth into the guest bedroom, and nodded toward the window. Stealthily, we crossed the room; she unlocked the window sash, and I eased it up just enough to overhear Eddie's conversation with Rhonda, even though we couldn't see them.

"What are you doing here, Rhonda?"

"We missed something. Ms. Doyle will be home later, and this was my chance to look around."

"How did you get in?"

"There was a key under the mat. Just like I told your friends. I didn't break in. I was cautious not to be seen."

"You were found performing an illegal search. Wearing civilian clothes as a police officer is taking it too far."

"Can I help it? I came up with the idea on the drive to the station."

Her tone was condescending. I could picture the corners of Eddie's mouth dipping in annoyance. It was a look he had given me several times in the first few days I was in town.

"What do you think we overlooked?"

"You said it yourself. This was such a mundane event. The perp took a cigar box when there were expensive jewelry pieces, antique pocket watches, and other items that would have been easy to slip into a bag. Why an old cigar box that Ms. Doyle had just unpacked?"

Beth nodded, and I had been thinking the same way.

Eddie said, "I was going to discuss this with you when you got in, but now that you've shown up here, you've encouraged the sofa sleuths to keep poking around."

"Who's that?"

I grinned. How would Eddie explain us to this overly zealous and stickler of a cop?

"Beth and Claudia."

"A woman who sews and one who knits for a living?"

I clenched my fists and punched the air. Who was she to look down her nose at our jobs? She wouldn't have warm sweaters or pretty clothes in her closet if it weren't for people like us. That didn't even include the fact that we were talented businesswomen.

He chuckled. "Don't underestimate those two. We had an involuntary manslaughter case and another murder about seven months ago, and without their input, we might never have caught a corrupt cop, and a woman could have gotten away with murder."

"Please tell me you didn't encourage them."

Ker Choo! I broke into a light sweat. Dang it, now we had to get out of here. Beth and I jumped up and rushed into Fiona's bedroom.

I smacked my hand to my forehead. "Shoot. I forgot to close the window."

7

———

"Claudia?" Eddie's footsteps were getting closer to the bedroom.

"Quick, open her closet." Beth pulled out straw hats, and I peered into the top drawer.

"Beth, we should bring a pair of sneakers. I'm not sure what Fiona was wearing when she was taken by ambulance."

Eddie filled the doorway, a pair of sunglasses stuck out from his shirt pocket. "Ladies, what are you doing?" I knew Rhonda must be behind him.

I gave him a forced smile and hoped it

looked natural for me. "You know. We're picking out clothes for Fiona. But she didn't say specifically what she wanted. What do you think, sneakers or shoes?"

He cocked a brow. "Either will be fine."

"Okay, sneakers it is." I removed socks and other garments from the drawer, closed it, and opened the next one, which contained yoga pants and butter-soft tee shirts. "Was there something else, Eddie?"

"How much longer will you and Beth be packing clothes?"

"Not long."

Beth said, "We're going to make lunch and dinner and pop them in the refrigerator so Fiona can get a quick meal when she's hungry."

That was a great idea to throw Eddie and Rhonda off the trail, and it would be a nice thing for Fiona, too.

Eddie looked at me. "Are you cooking?"

"Now, I know you're joking. We both

know that Beth is the kitchen wiz. I'll be her assistant and dishwasher."

"Will you lock up when you leave?"

I held out my hand. "If Rhonda would return the key."

I saw the smirk he tried to hide before he stepped aside to let Rhonda hand me the key.

"Make sure you do exactly as you said. I've got my eyes on the two of you." With one last look around the room, she stormed out, slamming the screen door after her.

Eddie walked into the spare room. I heard the window close before he returned. "The next time you decide to eavesdrop, keep from sneezing. If you feel one coming on, press your finger under your nose. It might stop it."

"Thanks for the tip."

He continued to hover.

"Was there something else?" My innocent act didn't fool him, but we were keeping up the pretense.

"Telling you to stop snooping is like

shouting at the moon. So, here's what I'll say off the record."

I felt my smile grow, and Beth's face morphed into a grin.

"If you find something, let me know. Do not go off on your own looking for answers. The person must have staked out the store to learn Fiona's routine, or so they thought. The locals know she's in her store late on Sundays. The perp wasn't local."

That was an interesting hypothesis and one we had already concluded. "They came for that box."

He nodded. "I don't know if we'll ever track them down, but that's what I believe."

"I wish Fiona had gotten a better look at the contents. Buying buttons is one thing that doesn't cause people to commit a crime."

He nodded. "Now, on the record. This is an official police investigation that, by all appearances, won't be closed for a long time. Please don't get involved and muddy the evidence."

"Us?" Beth asked. "We heard you tell Rhonda that we were helpful with your last big investigation." "You got lucky. Claudia turned that light on outside the shop during the day, and Uncle Ethan's not answering his phone alerted us that something was wrong. It doesn't happen like that every time there's an investigation."

"Are you saying you won't close the case and forget about it?" I hated that it sounded as if I was challenging him, but in some ways, I was.

"Rhonda was acting on a hunch."

"Or she's trying to cover her tracks. Maybe she's not the cop you think she is."

"Gigi, bad cops are rare. Just because you don't know her yet doesn't mean she won't be an asset on the force. And, just as a reminder, you didn't like me when we first met."

"Because you wanted to arrest me for murder?"

"I was doing my job, and it wasn't personal. Now look. We're great friends, and we're even going to go to the fall festival in Pembroke Cove together."

He made it sound almost like a date or was that wishful thinking? My heart skipped a beat, and I reminded myself I was not looking for romance. "Next time, don't be so gung-ho about your job."

Beth snickered. "You two need to stop bickering over old news. What's important is for Fiona to feel safe when she comes home and to know that you're still working the case."

"Before I go." He gave us each a stern look. "What other ideas did you have? I have my leads to chase, but it would be helpful if you get into a pickle and need help."

I had to give him something since saying we weren't going to do anything was an outright lie, and we'd both know it. "I want to take one final look in the shop, just to see if there's anything out of place or that doesn't belong. Then we'll be off to pick up Fiona."

He narrowed his eyes. "That's all?"

It wasn't a lie, but it also wasn't the complete truth. "Yes. To put your mind at ease, if we discover anything significant, I promise you'll be the first to know."

"Beth?"

"What Claudia said."

Plausible deniability for her was perfect.

"All right. Make sure you lock up, and if you get spooked, call or text. I'm not going out on patrol for another hour."

"Roger that." I smiled. "You know, there's one thing that might not amount to much: Fiona gave me the combination to a security box in the flower bed. However, the key was missing. She may have forgotten to put it back and instead placed it under the mat, but I thought you should know."

"I'll make a note of that. I'm curious: what was the combination?"

"It's a four-digit lock, and she used her shop phone number."

Eddie groaned. "The last four?"

I nodded. "Yeah."

He sighed. "I'll talk to her about that once she's feeling back to herself. Once again, try to convince her to install security cameras on the front and back doors."

Nodding I said, "I feel safer with mine."

Beth said, "I do, too. It's peace of mind if nothing else."

"All right. I'll check in with you later. Remember."

"I know. Call if there's one doodad out of place." Beth had placed a small tote bag on the bed, and I tossed in the garments I'd pulled from the dresser. "We're intelligent and capable women."

"That's what scares me."

After Eddie left, Beth and I finished filling the tote bag. I wasn't sure what Fiona would want to wear to be comfortable. "Since we said we would cook, we should whip up a few things."

Beth slung the tote over her shoulder.

"Tuna sandwich for lunch and a salad with grilled chicken for dinner."

"What makes you think those items are in the refrigerator?"

"If they're not, Polly's Pantry is right across the street."

We tossed together the tuna and had everything arranged on a dinner plate so that all Fiona would have to do was make the sandwich.

"I don't see any chicken." I closed the freezer door and opened the refrigerator. "No salad fixings either."

"Should we go to the store first and then search the shop and storage rooms or after?"

I looked at my watch and calculated how long both would take: "Polly's first, then the shop."

"Or we could divide and conquer. I'll go shopping, and you can look around downstairs."

Now that we had a plan, we went our separate ways. I took the inside stairs into the shop and flicked on the overhead lights to chase away the darkness in the lingering shadows. Also, if someone unknown was lurking, it was better for them to know where I was.

Whenever I felt uncomfortable, I talked. "Now then, to ensure the shop is ready to open later, I'd better check the front." I paused before I walked. The store was quiet. I strolled up and down each aisle, scanning them like I had the night before. I jiggled the unyielding doorknob. So far, everything remained unchanged.

"It's good to see that all's tidy. Now I'll check the back room." I paused again, straining to hear the slightest noise. While I had a prickling sensation down my spine, I shook it off as overactive nerves. "The storage room is next."

I flipped a few more light switches again, appreciating the similarity of our stores' layouts. Withdrawing my cell phone, I needed to take pictures of the shipping labels. Fiona was exceptionally organized. I could take a tip or two from her.

I spied the open cardboard box on the table. My heart quickened. This had to be the shipping container for the cigar box. I studied the label. Eureka. My first solid clue. I withdrew a slip of paper. "The paid invoice. Bucks and Bidding Auction Services. 'If you got the bucks we'll accept your bid.' How quaint."

I snapped a couple of pictures and noticed it said "box 1 of 4." I hesitated. Where were the others? I scanned the shelves of unopened boxes. Fiona had a lot of new inventory. "Ah ha!" There were the three I was searching for. However, she hadn't opened them yet. As much as I wanted to see the contents, perhaps that would have to wait until tomorrow. I took a picture of each label and placed the packing slip in the empty box. There wasn't much more for me to discover today.

I turned off the lights in the storage room and went to the back door to make sure I locked it. I wasn't surprised to see the deadbolt engaged, and the doorknob appeared new. I was certain it was Ethan's handiwork.

"All's good down here. I'm going back up to the apartment." I had to laugh at myself the entire time I'd been in the shop, and all the chattering I did, nothing stirred. "I'm just being silly. My imagination's in overdrive."

Jogging up the stairs, I closed the door and leaned against it. I gasped in surprise when I saw Rhonda in the doorway, this time in uniform. "What are you doing here, and how did you get in?"

She held up the key. "I forgot to give this to you when I left earlier."

"No, you gave me the key." I narrowed my eyes. "Do you have the extra key?"

She placed it on the table. "What were you doing downstairs? I thought you were cooking."

"Not that it's your concern, but I looked around one more time. I didn't want Fiona walking into any mess."

"Are you always so accommodating to others?"

"For people I like, I'm happy to help where possible." I picked up the key and slipped it into my pocket. "You didn't say what this key opens?"

"The deadbolt for the back door."

"How did you get it?"

She shrugged. "I was in the shop earlier and saw it was in the lock. I took it as a safety precaution. What if the perp breaks in again, sees the key, takes it, and makes a duplicate so they can get back in at any time?"

It didn't matter that she made little sense. "That's a solid door; no one could have seen it from the outside. Ethan left it there for Fiona. It wasn't yours to take, even though you're trying to justify your actions. I wonder what Eddie would think about your over-reaching?"

Her jaw twitched. "I'm a police officer investigating a theft and an assault. That makes it pertinent to my duties."

"And I'm Fiona's friend looking out for her best interests. I don't think the police can come and go as they please once a crime scene has been released."

"You should tread carefully as the concerned friend. I could arrest you and Beth for interfering with an active investigation."

"We have done nothing wrong." I hoped she was bluffing, trying to get me to spill my guts. But I lived in the city. I had a titanium spine. An overzealous cop trying to prove herself didn't scare me. Much. Especially after the Amos incident.

"What do you call deliberately listening to a private conversation between police officers?"

I thrust my chin up. "If it was a secret, perhaps you shouldn't have chatted on the deck and gone somewhere more private."

"You have an answer for everything, don't you, Ms. Grant?"

"The truth is, you couldn't stand me from the moment you laid eyes on me. I have no idea why. Is it because I'm friends with Eddie? We're not competing for anything."

"You need to watch yourself. I'll be keeping a close eye on you, and if I hear a whiff of information that you're in your *sofa sleuth* mode, I'll be all over you, and it will be the last time you think you're capable of doing anything remotely similar to police work. Do I make myself clear?"

"Officer, I would never assume I'm capable of doing your job. I'm a dress designer with a store where I sell my creations. I buy fabric, lace, buttons, and other materials to make clothes. Now, if I reach out to a vendor you find questionable or inappropriate to obtain those items, remember we both have jobs to do."

"Did you threaten me?"

"Of course not." I gave her a tight smile.

Beth rounded the kitchen corner and crossed her arms over her chest. "Rhonda, this is a surprise. I overheard most of this conversation, and as the daughter of the former chief of police, I can tell you that Claudia didn't threaten you. In fact, it might be the other way around, or should I say it's intimidation of a citizen?"

Despite Beth's voice being soft and controlled, I had seen the stern look in her eye when she dealt with Amos Brand, a former Drakes Bay policeman, at Colton Prescott's house. She wasn't a pushover.

"Beth." Rhonda looked between us. "I was returning a key I had forgotten to leave earlier."

"Claudia has the key."

I patted my pocket. "I do."

"Very good. Please understand this is a small town, and people gossip. Shop owners will talk about this since they're going to feel vulnerable. Claudia and I have the right to be a part of these conversations. We're not breaking any laws."

I was glad that Beth and I were friends; she was adept at weaving our cover story for when we questioned people in town about what they might have seen leading up to yesterday.

"Rhonda, thank you for the key. I'll let Fiona know that you may have questions for her later. But it would be great if you could wait until tomorrow."

Before I could finish my thought, she pushed dark glasses up her nose and turned. "Ladies." We heard her clomp down the stairs.

I hurried into the living room to look down Main Street, making sure she was gone. Rhonda turned and looked up.

I sagged against the wall. "She is one intense cop and doesn't like me at all. I wish I knew why."

8

───────

The soles of my sneakers squeaked against the hospital's linoleum floor, and disinfectant permeated the air. Beth and I stopped at the nurses' station. A petite, redheaded woman looked up from a computer screen.

"Good morning. We're here to pick up Fiona Doyle."

"Yes. She's getting her discharge paperwork and will be ready soon. You can go to her room if you'd like. It's 304."

I smiled. "Thank you."

Beth asked, "How much will you share with Fiona?"

"Nothing unless she asks, at least until we get her home. I don't want anyone to over-hear us."

Her eyes widened. "Surely no one at the hospital could be connected."

My steps slowed. "I don't want to take any chances. For all we know, Rhonda might pop up and insert herself into our con-versation."

"That's a true statement."

I tapped the door and opened it slowly. Fiona was sitting up in bed, gazing out the window.

"Good morning, Fiona."

"Girls." A smile lit up her face. "I'm so happy to see you. I didn't get a wink of sleep last night." With a flick, the blanket flew off, and she sat on the edge of the bed. With a gleam in her eye, she held out her hands and grinned. "Clothes for my escape."

"It's not like you're leaving against the doctor's orders."

"If I'm not wearing this backless dress, I won't look like a patient, either."

I passed her the bag. "Do you need help? All the tops we brought are pullovers. I didn't take your stitches into account."

"I'll be fine." She opened the bag. "How many outfits did you bring?"

"Four," Beth said.

Fiona laughed. "If you would close the curtain, I'm one step closer to getting out of here, and then you must tell me everything you know." She winked.

"We'll wait outside." I followed Beth out of the room and stood in front of the door.

Beth said, "She's feisty this morning."

"I hope I'm like her in another thirty years."

"You will be, since you already are."

I bumped her shoulder. "I've got excellent company. I don't know many people willing to track down clues in a crime."

"What can I say? It was fun the first time. Besides, since getting to know you, I don't want you going off and having all the fun."

I laughed. "A little scary, but it felt good to stretch the brain cells."

"Girls, I'm ready."

I turned and whispered to Beth, "That was fast. She wants out of here."

"I'll check with the nurse to see when we can leave if you want to help our patient relax."

Beth went to the nurses' station, and I entered the room. Fiona was sitting in a chair. On the bed was a clear plastic bag with what I surmised were her clothes from yesterday. I sat next to it.

"I'm sorry our dinner was cancelled."

"It's okay. We'll reschedule. Eddie has taken the cupcakes to the station as evidence and the butter brickle ice cream's in the freezer for you."

"Yum, butter brickle is my favorite." Her

words were cheerful, but her face tightened, and her eyes had lost their sparkle.

"Fiona, are you in pain?"

"A little headache. Nothing troublesome. I'm upset about the recent events."

I placed my hands on her shoulders. "I understand, but we should wait until we're in the car or at your place to discuss it."

She nodded. "I know. It's just the frustration of staying here overnight, waiting to leave when I only want to be in my own space, surrounded by good smells." She wrinkled her nose. "Not this place."

"It was important you receive proper care with a head wound."

She nodded.

Beth came in. "It'll be a few more minutes, and the nurse will bring in the paperwork. She said you saw the doctor earlier, so we're not waiting for him."

"He checked my head and said I was free to leave. That's when I started dreaming of the escape. I don't think he was out the door yet."

We all laughed, knowing how we were. Beth and I would have done the same thing had we been in the hospital bed.

I stashed the plastic bag in the tote bag. "Is there anything else that I should pack?"

"I travel light," she grinned. "As long as you girls aren't packing for me."

A nurse bustled in. "Fiona, you're all set. Is it okay if I review your discharge orders in front of your friends?"

"I have nothing to hide."

The nurse reviewed the details and concluded, "If you have any dizziness or worsening discomfort, contact your doctor or come to the emergency room."

Her brows knitted together. "Is that expected?"

The nurse placed her hand on Fiona's arm. "We don't. But we want you to know what is and isn't normal. I anticipate you should recover just fine. Rest when you need to, and don't overdo it when you open your store tomorrow."

"I'm opening today."

"I would advise you to take the day. Nap if you need it. Hospitals aren't known for getting a good night's rest."

"That's a true statement." Fiona took the papers, folded them in half, and stuffed them into the tote bag. "Girls, you heard the lady. Let's blow this ice cream stand."

Beth grabbed her tote as Fiona settled into the wheelchair. She realized that protesting would do no good since the nurse had mentioned it was policy.

"Beth, I'll take the tote if you want to pull your SUV up."

"Great idea. I'll see you out front."

Beth took the stairs while we waited for the elevator. I had questions, and Fiona did, too. How much should I tell her about Beth and my plan regarding the auction? Her hands were clasped in her lap as her jaw quivered.

"Is there much mess to clean up? Where you found me?"

"No. It's been taken care of." I held her hand while we rode the elevator to the ground floor.

"You resemble your uncle quite a bit. Sometimes, when I close my eyes, I feel as though he's still here with us."

I thought of his ghost waiting in the store for a full report on Fiona. "In some ways, I guess he's still with us."

The SUV's passenger door was open when the glass and metal doors slid aside. As soon as Fiona buckled in, she thanked the nurse and closed her door. Beth got behind the wheel, and I was in the back.

Once the car was in motion, Fiona said, "Tell me everything, and don't treat me like an injured woman. Someone broke into my store, and if I know you two, you've got a good theory."

Beth glanced her way. "Now, Fiona. Are you implying we're nosy?"

"On the contrary. You're intelligent young ladies with inquisitive minds. I heard the stories about you and Colton Prescott. Fill me in on everything."

"This is still an active investigation for the police, and we're not stepping on their toes." I needed to establish that right from the start. "However, Beth and I have been discussing our ideas while walking around the shop and your apartment several times."

Fiona turned in her seat. Her gaze flicked between Beth and me. "And?"

"When I arrived at your place yesterday, the door was unlocked. I knocked, but you didn't answer at first. Then I heard you call for help, so I entered and set the dessert I brought on the bench. That's when I discovered you in the store."

"I had a few minutes and wanted to tidy up. It's what I usually do, but I went downstairs early instead of doing it after supper. I wanted to grill the shrimp, so I wouldn't have to worry about the stove."

"Once the ambulance team took you to the hospital, Eddie accompanied me upstairs to explore. We know the intruder entered through the back door after picking the lock. In other news, Ethan installed a deadbolt on that door for added protection."

"I'll need to thank him." She pressed her fingers to her eyes. "What did you discover upstairs? Based on the story, I'm sure you discovered something. Did they find my safe?"

"I didn't know you had a safe, but they had gone through your desk. They must have been in the apartment when I entered since later, I discovered a cupcake was missing."

"They took a cupcake? Why on earth would they take the time for a snack?"

"In defense of the intruder, they were from Brewed Bliss."

She nodded. "Ah, that does make some odd sense. What do you suppose they were trying to find in the desk?"

"As nothing else seems out of place in the shop, meaning they only took the button box, we believe they were looking for packing slips for the three other boxes that came from the auction house."

"Were those opened?"

Beth said, "No, we think they were searching for something besides the buttons and didn't want to take the time or make it obvious that there was more for them to discover."

Clenching her hands in her lap, Fiona bowed her head. "Do you think this person would have left me bleeding on the floor?"

"I don't think so. Although they made a mess in your desk, they didn't trash the apartment or the store. What they did was criminal, but I found you, so they knew you were getting help."

She lifted her tear-filled eyes and looked at me. "How did they get away without being seen?"

"They went down the back stairs and through the alley between you and the inn.

We found the cupcake wrapper near the sidewalk on Main Street."

Her face brightened. "Someone might be able to identify this person?"

"Eddie's checking into the possibility, but he doesn't think so. Vacationers wouldn't have noticed anyone taking a perceived shortcut to the beach."

Beth asked, "Fiona, have you worked with that specific auction house previously?"

"Quite a few times. I've purchased several nice pieces of furniture and jewelry. This was the first time I bought four lots of boxes. There was a brief description of the antique buttons in one box. The other three are mystery lots. Like at the fair, you buy a paper bag, not knowing if you'll get an amazing treasure or a dud."

"But the packing slip would have more details about the contents of the boxes?"

"I'm sure it's for insurance purposes. As I mentioned, the auction was a couple of weeks ago, and I didn't unpack the boxes until yesterday, well one box." She frowned. "That doesn't help you with your dressmaking."

"It's fine. I never told the bride or her mother that I may have found something for their dress. Don't worry, I'll figure that out."

"That's one saving grace. I wouldn't want your customers to be upset with you because of my issue."

"Please, don't give it another thought; these are separate issues. Today is about you, and tomorrow, I'll dive into the button issue."

"What else can you tell me?"

"Rhonda Perkins, the new police officer, is a bit overzealous when it comes to us." I poked Beth on the shoulder, and she grinned. "You might want to keep us out of any conversations you have with the officer other than what happened yesterday."

"And what are your plans?"

"Not knowing what our plans are gives you plausible deniability."

"If you and Beth plan to look into something, please let me know. I might be able to help."

Beth said, "We're going to contact the auction company. We're not sure if they keep records of who bids on the items, but if we can find someone interested in the lots you purchased, it might give us a lead to follow."

She pinched the skin on her throat. "Isn't that something best left to the police?" A frown line appeared between her eyes.

"I'm searching for antique buttons, lace, and fabrics. The pretense I'll use is that you are purchasing items for me. If someone else is acquiring similar items, I may be able to contact them about items they want to sell."

"Oh." She perked up. "You're not going to say someone stole the buttons, but who else might be purchasing them?"

"Exactly, what estate did they come from? There could be more in storage or yet to be released."

"I never thought to ask if there were more items. After I have some decent coffee, would you like to help me unpack the three re-maining boxes? There might be an additional clue."

Beth flicked on a blinker. "Good coffee and muffins coming up." She eased into a parking spot behind Twice Loved. "I'll run across the street and pick up something de-licious."

"And I'll take Fiona upstairs so she can check her desk. It might reveal another clue that wouldn't have been obvious to us."

"I wish I was thirty years younger. Fol-lowing a trail of clues with you would be so much fun."

"Isn't that what we're about to do?" I got out with the tote bag and opened Fiona's door.

Beth locked the SUV and disappeared up the alley.

Fiona frowned. "I never realized how popular that alley could be. It provides quick access from the street to the back of our buildings and the bay." We slowly climbed the steps. Something was troubling her as she continued to take sidelong glances at me.

I withdrew the key from my pocket. "Fiona, you said I could find the house key in the security box in the flower bed. But it wasn't there, and I discovered Rhonda in your apartment early this morning. She said the key was under the doormat."

"I never put a key under the mat. It's like hanging up a sign to tell every criminal you've rolled out the welcome mat. The flower bed is bad enough, but at least it's in a locked container. Or was."

I took a deep breath and opened the door. This case just took an awkward twist. How could I tell a cop that I knew she lied about a key?

9

———————

Beth and I sat at Fiona's kitchen table while she scanned the packing slips from the boxes.

"There's not much detail. We're going to need to open them." She handed them to me and sipped her coffee. "Now, this is what coffee should taste like. Not that bitter brown water they tried to pass off as coffee in the hospital."

"You're home with good coffee and excellent sweets."

"And even better friends." She patted our hands. "If I haven't said it, thank you for everything."

"You're welcome. Now, let's get back to the details. There's nothing on this paper that indicates anything of interest."

Beth said, "That's probably why they left them."

"Or took pictures of them. Otherwise, we'd have a heads up if they planned a return visit."

Fiona drew back in her chair. "Is that even possible?"

"It is. Would you reconsider cameras? At least on the back doors? The street side has more activity, and we know the alley was used to break into my store. Installing them gave me a sense of peace I didn't know I needed."

"I just don't want people watching video clips of me coming and going."

"You have control of everything. It's not

like hiring a security company that monitors your property twenty-four/seven. You can share clips if needed; otherwise, you're the only person with access."

Her face brightened. "That's much different than I thought. Is it expensive?"

"Not really. There's a monthly subscription fee, and you purchase the cameras. They need to be installed, but overall, it's worth its weight in gold for peace of mind."

"Beth, would you call Eddie and ask him for recommendations? I want to install a few, and maybe I'll think about adding a couple inside for good measure."

She pushed back from the table. "I'll call Dad. It'll be quicker to get an answer since Eddie's on patrol."

A relaxed smile crossed Fiona's face. She placed a hand over her heart. "I never wanted to be one of those overly anxious people scared of the shadows, but this attack has shown me that being prepared isn't fear.

It's being smart." She pushed back from the table. "I'll be right back, and then we'll open the remaining boxes. Maybe they'll have a clue as to what might have been in the cigar box that was so important."

I was sipping coffee and perusing the packing slips when I looked closer.

Box 1. Shirt and dress buttons.
Box 2. Misc. fabrics.
Box 3. Gloves and hats.
Box 4. Costume jewelry.

I was excited to see the contents of boxes two and three. There might be treasures I'd be happy to take off Fiona's hands. But box one was the mystery. Antique buttons could be expensive, but were they worth stealing a box and assaulting a woman? I pulled out my phone and tapped the *Cost of Vintage buttons* in the search bar.

Scrolling, I saw resale sites and auction

houses that specialized in buttons and links on the history of buttons.

"Whatcha looking at?" Beth sat down in a chair. I handed her my phone.

"Button information. Per the shipping papers, it was a box of buttons. I was wondering how much buttons are worth. It doesn't seem there's anything worth going to jail for."

She handed me the phone. "There's a link to a well-known auction house you'll want to check out later. Buttons can be expensive if encrusted with jewels or precious metals."

Fiona came into the room. "I'm ready."

"Half a sec. I was looking at the papers again. Did you see the contents of the boxes before you bid on them, or was there just a description on the website?"

Pursing her lips, she tapped them. "I participate in many auctions. What did I see this time?" With a snap of her fingers, she said, "I know. I saw a picture. They didn't show a live view. It's a bit unusual, as most people who attend online won't bid unless the image is live, but there was a pretty assortment of silver, bone, and, of course, the costume variety. Inexpensive pearls, too."

"There were gemstones?" I glanced at Beth; she was also hanging on to Fiona's description.

"Even with antique items, paste stone was commonly used. It provided the allure of wealth. During the Art Deco period, after the great crash of 1929, if a stone was lost in a piece of jewelry, it was common to replace it with synthetic or glass. Money didn't flow freely, even for the wealthy, although they tried to maintain the façade."

"Could any of the buttons you purchased be real?"

"Doubtful. The box was under thirty dollars. From what I've been told, all items are inspected by a qualified antiques dealer before the auction. They set a minimum bid if the item is valuable; when it's not, there's no reserve. Or the estate wants everything gone, and a large cash settlement is the driving force."

"Costume or low-value metals wouldn't be attractive to a thief. Is it likely something was slipped inside before shipping it to you?"

"I suppose anything's possible. Sadly, there's no way to know since it's gone."

Beth and I stood and tossed the coffee cups into the trash. A few muffins remained in the bag, so I placed it on the counter. I wished Fiona had checked the boxes when they arrived, but I couldn't turn back the clock to make things different.

Three hours later, I was in my workroom with a box of antique lace from one of the auction boxes. Fiona had been happy to part with it.

Beth sat in my desk chair.

"I'm ready to call Bucks and Bidding."

"You're sticking to the questions about items like what Fiona bought?"

"Yes, and from the same estate. I need to figure out a way to ask if there was a lot of competition for the boxes she bought. I'm not sure how to get into that."

Beth smiled. "Tell them you bought the box of lace from Fiona's shop, and you're hoping to find more."

Herman floated into the room. "How's Fiona?"

"That seems like the best approach. She said it was a great idea when I mentioned it to her."

"I'm relieved she's going to be all right."

Pausing mid-fold, "She's a tough lady. I think she's more upset that I don't have the buttons than she is about getting broken into."

"When I spoke to Dad, he thought Beau Tinker would stop first thing in the morning and give her a day to install the cameras."

"That is good news. Since I've had them, I

can't tell you the number of times I heard a strange noise and checked to discover it was just the wind."

"Just wait until you hear a snowplow in the middle of the night. It sounds like nails on a chalkboard with lots of thumping."

"Great. Something to look forward to this winter."

Beth's cell pinged, and she stood. "I'm going to take off. There's a salesperson at the store I forgot was coming. Let me know what you learn from the auction house."

"You got it. Better yet, do you want to come by later. We'll chat about the clues?"

Her expression shifted. "I can't. I have a date with Luke tonight."

I wiggled my eyebrows. "I had no idea, and he's good looking. Where are you going?"

"Dinner and a walk on the beach. I plan to ask him if he wants to join us for the fall festival. Eddie mentioned that he wanted to go."

"Are you trying to set me up with Eddie?"

She placed a hand over her heart and said, "Who me?" Then she giggled. "You're cute together, and don't forget he calls you Gigi. That has to mean he's a little interested."

"Or he likes to poke at me because he finds me annoying."

"Just like in school when a boy would pull your hair." She winked. "I'll bring breakfast, and we can catch up before our shops open."

"Have fun tonight. I'll brew the coffee if you want to grab egg sandwiches."

"What time?"

"Seven-thirty? If that's too early, we can do it later."

Beth grinned. "It might be earlier if the date is a bomb." She sauntered through the shop, and I heard the bell above the door jingle when she closed it.

Herman zipped around the room. "Finally, you can talk freely." When he perched on the desk, he gave me a grave look. "Fiona will recover from being attacked?" His transparent hand went to the back of his head.

"She will, and thankfully, it wasn't as bad as your injury, and she got help right away."

He bowed his head. "That's a relief."

In the last six months, there had been many times I wished I could give him a comforting hug. The next best thing was to discuss details about the business. "Herman, did you often purchase auction items from Fiona or directly from auctions?"

"A little of both. I'll assume you believe the attack is linked to the auction."

"To state the obvious, yes. I've researched antique buttons, and while they can be valuable compared to jewelry, they're just a drop in the bucket. In the past, I've used vintage buttons in my designs. The highest amount I've ever paid for them was in the mid-double digits."

"You use such quaint sayings." He drifted around the room and peered at the box of lace. "This is nice."

"Fiona bought four boxes, and we looked in the three she hadn't opened. Only two would have caught my interest: the cigar box, fabrics, and costume jewelry. I asked if she had seen pictures or if it was a live auction, and she confirmed she only saw pictures."

"It's possible that someone slipped a valuable item into the box before shipping, thinking they could retrieve it once it arrived at its final destination."

"If only I had pictures of the cigar box contents. I could look online to see if any items looked valuable."

"Well, you don't. So, stop talking about it and take action."

I grabbed my phone from the table, and I hated to admit it, but Herman was right. I had these thoughts swirling around in my head, and they weren't moving me forward. After writing down the number from the image on my phone, I dialed. When no one picked up and the answering machine didn't respond, I wondered if I had the wrong number.

I redialed. On the second ring, I heard a rushed "Hello. Bucks and Bidding."

Tapping the speaker phone button so Herman could hear, I said, "Hello. This is Claudia Grant. I hope you can give me some information on recently auctioned items."

"No refunds."

"That's not the question."

"Good. You have no idea how frequently customers experience buyer's remorse when their shipment arrives."

"I'm calling about a couple of boxes you shipped to Twice Loved in Drakes Bay, Maine, to Fiona Doyle."

"Then you should speak with Ms. Doyle. Not me."

"I've purchased the fabric box from your auction and hoped to find more. Is it possible to know who asked you to auction those items?" My heart skipped. It was the truth, but this man was less than cordial.

"You're looking for similar items? Why?"

"I'm a dress designer who often incorpo-

rates vintage fabrics and buttons. I'm currently working on a bridal gown for which
I'm sourcing vintage buttons. I'm hoping to
find sea pearls."

He snorted. "Who's this dress for? They'll
need deep pockets if you search for antique
sea pearl buttons. They're rare and expensive.
Maybe they want seed pearls—just as nice
and budget-friendly."

"I believe the box of buttons Fiona purchased had sea pearls."

"Nothing like that has ever come
through my auction house. I get quality
antiques or paintings but scarce gems?
Nope. Not happening. I'm a small
business."

"Could it happen that rare items got
mixed in with your typical items?"

"If they did, you can be sure I'd extract
full value at auction. All boxes are vetted
prior to the sale."

I wasn't getting anywhere fast. This man
was adamant nothing had slipped into

Fiona's box. "Are you expecting more items from that estate?"

"Anything is possible, lady."

"Claudia Grant."

"Right. Do you want me to put you on my list of upcoming events?"

Herman bobbed his head.

"That would be helpful." After I gave him my email address, I figured I'd try one more time. "Is it possible to get the name of the person who asked you to auction the fabric and buttons?"

"That would cut me out of my commission. Doesn't seem ethical."

"Look." I slapped my hand on the table. "What's your name?"

"Elias Nobilski."

"Elias. I give you my word—I won't purchase anything they plan to auction. And if they have something of interest, I can tell you that I'd like to participate in the event."

"Hmm. I don't know…"

I heard the hesitation in his voice. "I'm a

small business owner. I won't and don't condone unethical behavior to others."

The line was silent. Did this mean he was considering my request? Should I push him to answer or wait?

Herman was sort of patting my hand as if encouraging me to be patient for a moment or two.

"Claudia, is it?"

"Yes. Claudia Grant. I own Grants Gowns."

"So you said. I'm not a trusting sort of man. I've been burned more times than I care to count. However, in this instance, since you purchased the box from a good customer, I'll share with you where the lot originated. How old are you?"

That question was surprising. "I appreciate this, Elias, and I'm twenty-eight."

"Huh. You promise not to go behind my back and buy anything that might hurt my chances of making money with a new auction?"

"I give you my word." I held my hand to high-five Herman as his hand passed through mine with a chill.

"You also have to swear you won't tell them I gave you their name or phone number. Again, I need to protect myself."

"Then why are you agreeing?" Not that I wanted him to change his mind, but Elias seemed to be struggling to divulge the information.

"Sounds like you're just starting in business. When I started business as a young man, someone gave me a helping hand. I like to pay it forward when I can."

The buildup was poking on my last nerve. "I agree helping others is important." I didn't want to tell him I was tracking down a criminal.

"The items were from the Madison family over in New Castle."

"I'm not familiar with New Castle, Maine."

"That's because the town of New Castle is

in New Hampshire on the border with Maine."

My latest bride was from New Hampshire. *Did any of them mention what town?*

"Thank you, Elias. I appreciate the information." I hung up and glanced at Herman. "Do you think my bride's future husband's family may be connected to the missing button box?"

10

I walked over to the desk and powered on the old computer. The contact information for the bridal party stared back at me. Julia's future sister-in-law, Sienna Madison, was from New Castle, New Hampshire. I took a seat. My mantra, *there is no coincidence*, was staring me in the face.

"Herman, does this seem plausible?"

He slid next to me. "If you tell me, I can give you advice."

"Right. I was organizing my thoughts

about these buttons." I twirled in the desk chair. "Julia, my bride, has a family heirloom: her grandmother's dress, which is to be re-made into her bridal gown. It's missing all the buttons, but the rest of the gown is intact. What if someone from her family took the buttons off to replace them but never got around to it, and they ended up in the box that went to auction?"

"If it was, why don't you ask her if there are any pictures of what the buttons looked like? Photographs were around in the late nineteenth century. It's possible there were pictures."

I smacked my hand to my forehead. "Never mind that train of thought; her fi-ancé's family auctioned the boxes."

"You could research what type of buttons were used on wedding gowns from that time period. It might help you determine the value of what could have been used."

I nodded and turned back to the computer. Research was my thing. Tapping the keys, I brought up a history of wedding dresses. "It says that before World War II, only wealthy people wore white wedding gowns, which was deemed impractical since it was typical for a woman to own one special dress for her lifetime, and even then, it might be borrowed from a friend or relative. Mother of Pearl buttons were used throughout the Victorian era. Even if there were buttons from this period in that box, it hardly seems worth stealing."

"People are motivated by things we can't understand. However, it does seem odd." Herman drifted into the front room. "Claudia. Customer."

I waited for the door to open before entering the main salon. "Julia, this is a surprise. I was thinking about you."

She smiled. "That's nice to hear. I was looking at different venues for the reception to narrow down the options. Since I was in the area, I thought I'd stop by. I'm not interrupting your work, am I?"

"Not at all." I gestured toward a sofa. "Please sit. I was going to call you tomorrow to discuss the dress."

Her face lit up. "It's lovely, isn't it? Well, it will be after you're finished with it. I'm going to feel beautiful when I marry Tristan."

"You are beautiful. A dress will only enhance it."

A blush crept up her face. "Thank you."

"How can I help you today?"

"You said you would call me about the buttons. Have you found any replacements yet?"

"Nothing vintage. I have some suitable options if you'd like to take a look at them and select one."

She shook her head. "No, we've got time. Could you try some antique shops, or maybe that cute second-hand shop in town may have the perfect buttons?"

"I've checked, and she doesn't have any-thing that will work. However, I've asked Fiona to look out for something special."

"That's good." Her face fell. "I thought for sure it would be easier to replace them."

"Don't give up hope; we'll find the perfect ones." I patted her leg. "Besides, as you said, we have plenty of time before your special day. Until then, we can do fittings and finish the dress. Buttons are the final touch, anyway."

"It's just that," she clasped her hands and stared at them, "Sienna, my soon-to-be sister-in-law has discouraged me from wearing the dress. She said it's not right that I didn't buy a new gown."

"It's your choice, Julia. Not Sienna's. If she wanted to wear a vintage gown, would you object?"

"Oh, definitely not. Between my family and hers, we have trunks full of vintage clothes. I would have been thrilled if she and Betsy had chosen that option. There were plenty of cool items for the ladies to select from. It would have made for great photos. I want everyone to be happy. My mother is the most challenging one, as you saw."

"Your mother only wants what makes you happy."

"I guess." Julia shook my hand. "Thank you for your time. When should I plan to come back for a fitting?"

Hoping to spend more time with her to understand the conflict between her and Sienna, I suggested, "Tomorrow? If you're available."

"I can be here at ten. Should I bring the gang?"

"There's no need. We'll work on your gown, and if you have other ideas you'd like to incorporate, we can discuss them."

Her smile widened. She threw her arms around me and hugged me tightly. "Thank you, Claudia. I knew coming to your shop was the best decision."

"You haven't seen my work on your dress yet."

With a sweeping arm gesture, she said, "There's your work; that's all I need to see. In fact, before I leave, I'm going to shop." She winked at me. "I need honeymoon clothes."

"I can alter most everything, not just the hems."

She nodded her head toward the racks. "I'll browse."

I stepped back and allowed her to access the clothes without pressure. "I'll be in the workroom if you need help."

"Thank you." She focused on the garments as I slipped into the back.

Herman stretched across my worktable. "What are you doing?" I glanced over my shoulder to confirm Julia hadn't heard me.

He jabbed his finger at her. "I think she was aware of the buttons and, for some strange reason, took them."

"Why?" I moved to the opposite side of

the table to see if Julia became curious about who I was talking to.

"Come on. Julia has a wedding dress that needs vintage buttons. Her future family auctioned them off, which made her temper flare. In a fit of spite, she took them; however, things escalated, and she hurt Fiona. Case closed."

"Your theory is neat and tidy, but she could have bought the box from Fiona on Monday morning when the shop reopened. There's no motive for the theft other than your imagination."

"We need the marker board you have upstairs to review what you know so far."

I shook my head. "No."

Julia looked up. "Did you say something?"

"I was talking to myself." I didn't give the ghost my stink eye even though I wanted to.

She smiled. "Genius at work. I get it." She ran her hand down the row of garments. "I wish I had your talent. I've never seen love-lier dresses."

"Is there something you'd like to try on?"

With a glance at her wrist, she shook her head. "Tomorrow, when I come back for the wedding dress, I'll try on a couple of my favorites. Sadly, I have an appointment with another venue."

"If we run out of time, I'll be here Monday through Friday and Saturday by appointment." I walked her to the door. "I'll stay on top of the buttons too. Try not to give it another thought."

She smiled. "I know the dress is in good hands. See you tomorrow."

I watched her walk to her car and get inside. She sat there for several minutes before driving away. *What was she doing? Confirming directions to her appointment or calling someone?* I wished I had a better view.

Beth was hurrying in my direction. With a glance at Julia as she drove past, Beth held up two to-go cups. "I needed a break."

I met her halfway and took a cup. "Thanks. Did you notice if Julia was on the phone?"

Beth's brow creased. "Her mouth was moving, so I guess she was talking. When you sing to the radio, your head usually is moving in time to the music."

"That's an interesting observation."

We walked into the shop, and she flopped into one of the overstuffed chairs. I liked to consider it the FOB, or father-of-the-bride, chair.

"How was your meeting?"

"Good. That's what I wanted to talk to you about. He was an accessory rep, and it was an excellent opportunity to ask about vintage buttons. It's Percy's thing."

"I'm guessing Percy is the vendor?"

"Yes. Anyway, not only does he sell notions, which include new buttons, but I discovered he's an avid collector of vintage. I thought he knew it was because of his business, but it's the other way around. He only sells buttons because he's a collector. Sometimes, when he goes into shops, there are old garments with—"

I interrupted. "Old buttons. How does this help us?"

"I asked him why someone would want to steal a box." She sipped her coffee with her eyes sparkling above the cup.

Keeping me in suspense wasn't funny. Despite wanting her to spill the beans faster, I waited and tried to appear nonchalant.

With a laugh, she leaned forward and set her cup aside. "Percy said that most people assume vintage buttons that look like jewels are made of paste and that seed pearl buttons aren't valuable. They don't realize that what appears to be paste can actually be a real emerald, diamond, or another precious gem. There have been documented cases where gaudy buttons were produced to smuggle the real deal."

"I've never heard of such a thing. Are you sure he's telling the truth?"

"Think about it. A hideous broach worn on a lapel wouldn't get a second look, but it could contain a precious gem. It would be an effortless way to smuggle items."

"Are you saying that old buttons in a cigar box could have been put up for auction by mistake, and the family jewels were sitting in plain sight for who knows how long?"

Her head nodded. "Or there may have been some old coins mixed in, too. That's my thought, not his. I didn't mention the missing box to him. I mentioned that you were looking for vintage buttons and asked how much they might cost."

"We're no closer to solving this mystery. We know someone desired whatever was in the box. It ended up at auction by mistake, and the boxes Fiona purchased originated from the Madison estate in New Castle, New Hampshire. My bride, whom you saw leaving, is marrying into that family."

She let out a low whistle. "That's not a coincidence, which explains why you were curious if she was on the phone. Do you think she was here trying to dig up the dirt on what happened at Twice Loved?"

"She mentioned the store in passing, almost too casual. Asking if I could find vintage buttons at antique stores or the, and I quote, cute store in town."

"Is it your job to go antiquing to find buttons?"

"Not really. I look for vintage clothes and accessories that I can refresh, but it's more of a hobby than a regular part of my business."

"Maybe she should be trying to source buttons."

I held up a finger. "I've got an idea."

I entered the workroom, and Herman wasn't hanging around. I'm sure my conversation with Beth wasn't as captivating since he couldn't be a part of it, drifting off to wherever he went when I was working. I found my phone under the stack of lace and returned to the salon.

"I'm going to call Julia."

Beth arched a brow. "I can't wait."

Scanning my recent call list, I tapped the redial and speaker buttons. She answered on the first ring with a breathless, "Hello."

"Julia, hello. This is Claudia."

"Oh, hello. I'm surprised to hear from you. Do you have to cancel our appointment for tomorrow or did I leave something in the shop?"

"Not at all. After you left, I started thinking that as you're driving around the area looking for wedding venues, there are quite a few antique shops nearby. If you have time, you could drop into a few and check for buttons. I'll need at least ten to fifteen and more if you can find them."

Beth grinned and gave me an air high five.

"I'm, I'm not sure if I'd know what to buy."

"We're looking for pearl buttons, around seven to nine millimeters would be ideal."

"All right. I'll make the time to stop in a

couple. But isn't this something you should do?"

Beth smothered a laugh at the haughty tone in Julia's voice.

"Typically, when customers ask me to update a vintage garment, they supply all the items, or I use what I can obtain, which means the buttons won't be of the same era. If that's unimportant to you, I can use my normal vendor."

"That's okay. I can look, and I'll send a text message to my family and friends if anyone has their grandmother's sewing baskets lying around. Who knows what they might contain."

"That would be extremely helpful. If you can't find appropriate replacement buttons, I'll do my best to find some that are suitable."

"Thank you, Claudia. See you tomorrow," she disconnected.

"That set one thing in motion." I wanted to discuss Herman's idea with Beth. "Could it be possible that Julia knew her future in-laws were auctioning those items off and broke in to steal them?"

"Wait, what?"

"I was going to tell you in the morning." I updated her on what Elias from Bucks and Bidding shared. "What if Julia found out, became upset with them, and chose to take matters into her own hands, breaking in and stealing the box?"

"That's over the top. She could have asked you to purchase them or bought them herself."

"That's what I was thinking." At least we agreed that Herman's idea was farfetched. "Don't you have a date tonight?"

"Yes, but coffee with you is always interesting. Especially when we've got our super sleuth capes off the hanger."

I laughed. "Capes aren't in style this time of year."

She stood. "I'll see you bright and early, and you have to tell me everything you find out since we both know you can't let this go."

I sat there after Beth closed the door, smacking the arm of the sofa. *I never asked Fiona to see the pictures of the boxes she had gotten from the auction house.*

I dialed her number. When she answered, I said, "Fiona, it's me. Would you mind if I stopped by to look at the pictures you got from the auction house? I'm very interested in the button box."

11

"Claudia, I'm drained. Would you mind if I emailed the pictures to you?" Fiona's voice sounded weak.

"Do you need something? I could run to the store or the pharmacy for you."

"No. The dinner you left will be fine. I just need to rest. Before I lie down, I'll email you. Have you found out who might have done this?"

"Not yet. Have you spoken with Rhonda or Eddie since you've been home?"

"Yes. Unfortunately, the lady police officer

came by. She's quite rude. Why the town hired her is beyond me."

"She has excellent credentials, and I'm sure she wants to prove her worth. We should give her the benefit of the doubt."

"You're right, but she kept asking the same question repeatedly. Why would someone want the cigar box and nothing else from the store? I showed her the pictures, and she pushed me again about what was inside."

"You said you looked in the box. Did you compare it to the pictures from Bucks and Bidding?"

"No, there wasn't enough time. I glanced at the box when I picked it up, but then, you know what happened."

I didn't want her to dwell on the assault. "It's all right. The police will find and arrest the guilty person."

"With your help, I'm sure." Fiona laughed softly. "You have a mind for sifting through details and looking either closer to or at a distance from something to ferret out the truth."

"That's sweet, but I'm not in the caliber of trained professionals."

"Sometimes, the so-called professionals must follow rules that you don't, which is why you figured out who killed that curmudgeon, Prescott."

"I try to offer my help when it's needed." I needed to steer her away from my investigation. The less Fiona knew about my actions, the better. "I'm going to let you rest."

"Give me a few minutes and check your email. I'll send over everything I have from the auction."

"Thank you, and if you need anything at all, please call. Even if it's the middle of the night."

"You really are so like Herman. He'd say the same thing when I had so much as a sniffle."

"I'm glad you and Herman had one another. I'll give you a call tomorrow. Sleep tight."

"Good night, Claudia."

I remained seated while I contemplated my conversation with Fiona. Rhonda fixated on being the proverbial dog with a bone. But could Fiona have noticed something she didn't realize? It was possible. I might never know for sure. However, examining the images could help me add details to my clue board.

I secured the store and double-checked the back entrance before heading upstairs to my apartment. Lola trotted into the kitchen to greet me, weaving around my ankles. I knelt on the floor and pulled her close. "What do you think about our new case?" She purred and nuzzled her head, resting it against my chin. "I agree; we'll solve the mystery of the missing button box."

I set her on the chair and filled her food and water bowls before taking my laptop into the living room and opening Fiona's email. She had attached three pictures. One showed the box propped open, containing a mixture of pretty shell buttons, seed pearls, and crocheted rounds. The next image appeared to be from auction day, and the buttons were different; some paste rounds had surfaced. At least, that was my guess since the sparkly diamond version hadn't been visible before. The final picture showed it packed in a shipping box.

I sent them to the printer and listened as the paper progressed, ejecting printed copies. Before they were done, I cracked the windows in the front and back of the apartment to get a cross breeze. With the printer finished, I taped them to the side of the whiteboard. Herman appeared next to me.

"What do you see?"

I shook my head. "Not a thing. You?"

"What if whoever packed the shipping box added something to the buttons after the photos were taken?"

"Trying to smuggle something out of the auction house?"

He zipped around and settled on the window seat. "It's what I would do if there were something valuable I was trying to steal, like a ring or pair of earrings."

"I've been so focused on buttons that it never crossed my mind that it could have been something entirely different. This means that whoever slipped something into the box knew where it was going and had to wait for the opportune moment to sneak in and try to retrieve it. But why wait a couple of weeks?"

"Claudia, you're asking questions that relate to a devious mind. You need to think like that type of person."

I paced in a circle around the living room. "There must have been something in that box by mistake. I don't want to think someone was smuggling items out of the auction house. I need to speak to Sienna Madison since it was her family, but I can't just call her up and say, *'Hey Sienna, did someone in your family put something in an auction, and did someone else knock a woman out to get it back?'*"

"Well, you could, but that's not advisable."

"Herman, I should leave this to Eddie and Rhonda and not get my socks in a twist."

A sharp rap on my door stopped my pacing. "Who could that be?"

"A funny thing happens when you answer the door. You'll find out."

I flashed my ghost a frown. "You think you're funny?"

"Hilarious." He crossed his ghostly arms and nodded to the door.

I rounded the archway and saw Eddie standing on the deck with his back to me. After opening the door, I said, "This is a surprise."

He turned, holding a pizza box and a brown paper bag. "Dinner?"

I stepped back and held the door. I would have said, *"Come on in. I never turn down takeout,"* if I had felt bold, especially when a handsome man delivered. But that was inappropriate; we were just friends.

"I hope you don't mind, but I thought you were working on your clue board. And before you say you're not, I'm kind of hoping you are."

My brows arched to my hairline. "Really?" I closed the door. "Won't Rhonda be annoyed that you're talking to me? She's clarified that I need to keep my nose out of this." I follow him into the kitchen.

He placed the box and bag on the table. "That's only because she is trying to prove her worth to the police force. Involvement of a civilian in the case can complicate her efforts to make a good impression."

"And you won't tell me to stay out of it? The last time we were in a similar situation, that's what you said several times."

"True, but you're not in the line of fire this time. Using your brain's superpower, once it's been fueled by an everything pizza and Greek salad, is a brilliant move on my part."

I laughed, asking as I withdrew plates from the cabinet. "Beer, wine, soft drink?"

"Coffee, if you don't mind? I'm on patrol tonight."

I measured out enough for four cups and started the pot. "Do you want to see my board?"

He grinned. "Of course. Should we eat first?"

I handed him a plate, napkin, and fork. "This calls for eating in the other room."

Once we settled, he scanned my notes. "Where did you get the pictures from the auction house?"

"Fiona sent them over a while ago. It's part of the process when she attends a virtual event. As you can see, the first and second pictures show slightly different contents, but I think that's because the box was shaken. We won't see the contents again until Fiona unpacks them. My current idea is that someone slipped something in before the box shipped and planned to retrieve it once it arrived at Twice Loved."

"Did Fiona say if there was something in the box that she wasn't expecting?"

"She only did a quick peek, figuring we'd sort through the buttons over dinner."

"Why did you want them?"

"I'm restoring a vintage wedding dress for a client. The dress is missing its buttons, and I wanted to be authentic. When Fiona mentioned that she had some, I was intrigued." *Should I share the connection between Sienna Madison and the auction?* "As a side note: the boxes came from the Madison estate, the same family and town as the husband-to-be."

"That's interesting. Have you asked anyone about the connection?"

"Not yet. I want to know what's in the box. I'm not sure how to casually bring it up in conversation. The bride is returning tomorrow for a fitting, so that might be the opportunity I'm looking for."

"Do you think her future in-laws will be with her?"

I shrugged. "Possible, but the attendants won't have a fitting for a few weeks. The bride's dress has my full attention. Eddie, do you think Rhonda has an ulterior motive regarding this case?"

"Why do you ask?"

"I found her in Fiona's apartment dressed in street clothes, and I'm sure she used the key from the hiding place. That's not something an officer would do, as it could bring any evidence found into question, right?"

He gave a thoughtful nod. "She's a good cop, but it sounds like she's suffering from a case of overzealousness."

"You don't think she could be the one who broke into Twice Loved and was pretending to investigate while we discovered her in Fiona's apartment? Why wouldn't she be in uniform and have a partner if she were doing her job?"

"Good questions. I'm going to ask her what is going on. She can't mess up the case."

Shifting on the sofa, I said, "Any chance you can avoid mentioning the information came from me? She's already holding a grudge."

"I'll figure out how to work it into a conversation and do my best to keep you out of it."

"I appreciate that."

His tone was nonchalant, "The fall festival should be fun. Beth's looking forward to it."

"It will be fun. I'm curious, are she and Luke close?"

He arched a brow. "As in a couple?"

I avoided his penetrating gaze. "Did you go to school together?"

"We did. Beth had a crush on him when we were kids, but he was too self-absorbed to notice."

Bang! Bang! Gunshots. I jumped to my feet, my heart thumping in my chest. Herman was whizzing toward the shop door. Eddie was one step behind me.

I raced down the interior steps, skimming the handrail, and jumped the bottom three while looking right and left. Silence surrounded me. I pointed to the back door, and Herman's ghostly form made its way to the salon.

Eddie grasped my hand. "Allow me to go first." But my fingers had flipped the dead-bolt and flung the door wide open. Nothing seemed out of place.

Laughter drifted toward us—I guessed from the beach. We looked at each other and moved around the back of the inn. Our steps slowed as we reached the back entrance of Twice Loved. Shattered on the step was a pane of glass from a wood window. Eddie turned the door handle. "It's locked."

I looked up the stairs to Fiona's apartment. Taking them two at a time, Eddie and I raced up. "Fiona!" I banged on the back door. Twisting the knob, I found it locked. I remembered Rhonda saying she had found a key under the mat. I flipped it back, but there was nothing. I pounded on the wood frame. "Fiona, are you all right?"

I paused, willing the sound of footsteps to

reach us. Could she be lying in another pool of blood? I raised my fist again, but I heard the faint sound of shuffling steps.

Fiona appeared, confusion etched on her face. "Claudia, Eddie. What are you doing here?"

"We heard what sounded like fireworks or gunshots at my place and rushed over here." I wrapped my arms around her and held on tightly.

"I'm fine, I was in my office tidying things up."

I walked her outside the door and pointed to the back step. "Look."

She sucked in a breath. "Whose window is that?"

"Good question." Eddie said, "I'm going to call this in. He stepped to the rail, and I couldn't hear what he was saying, which was fine. I figured I'd know the gist of the conversation. He slipped his phone into his jeans pocket. "A couple of officers are on their way."

"Rhonda?"

"No, she's off duty."

That was a relief. If I could avoid it, I didn't want to deal with her again this week or month.

"Fiona, you don't know why someone would break an old window by your door?"

"No. I want to check the shop if you don't mind?"

He nodded as her statement turned into a question. "That's a good idea, but when we ran by the door, I tried the knob, and it was locked."

"The best news I've had so far. You know this might be some kids playing a prank."

Eddie looked at the corners of the building. "Have you spoken with someone about security cameras?"

"Beau Tinker's coming on Thursday." She clasped my hand. "Do you think this has something to do with the break-in?"

I glanced at Eddie, who shook his head at me. Fiona focused on me, so she didn't notice it. "No. It's like you said, probably some kids with nothing to do decided to play a prank."

A police cruiser stopped in the parking lot. Eddie said, "I'll go tell them what we know. Take Fiona inside, and we'll go into the shop from the apartment as soon as the officers on duty are ready."

I opened the door, and Fiona walked in ahead of me. Whispering, I asked, "Do you think this was a schoolkid's prank?"

He held my gaze. "Do you?"

"No. I'm going to ask her a few questions to see if she might have seen or heard anything unusual. Is that okay?"

"I'd rather you waited for me. This way, she won't have to repeat the story more than once. She's been through enough and has only been home from the hospital for less than a day, and now this."

"All right." My shoulders slumped. I was disappointed and didn't attempt to hide it.

"If she gets chatty before I get back, pay close attention to every detail," he winked.

"Consider me all ears." I paused. "Maybe someone was caught on the cameras at the inn or even something from my exterior views. Ethan certainly installed enough to capture many angles."

He nodded. "I was thinking the same thing." Halfway down the stairs, he looked back. "You know this has just taken a different turn, and whoever is responsible is more than likely tied to the burglary."

"That's why it's so important to find out who knew the box had been shipped here, and what else was at the auction house that might have been slipped inside." A chill raced down my spine. "Fiona isn't safe. Not until we have answers."

12

An hour later, we found nothing in Fiona's shop. However, we discovered evidence of firecrackers in the parking area near the beach. It might have been a gunshot, but I agreed with Eddie that it was more likely fireworks.

He and I climbed the back stairs to my place. I crossed to the railing and gazed across the parking area at the bay. "What was that all about?"

He shook his head. "I have no idea. But it doesn't make sense some kids would drag an old window to Fiona's back door and break it."

"No, it doesn't. What if they were testing to see if anyone would notice vandalism in broad daylight or if she was home?"

"I hope it's just bored kids," he said, glancing at the wall clock. "I need to leave to get ready for work." He nodded at the board. "Where are you headed from here, since we both know you won't forget about the case?"

"At first glance, it seems to be a simple case of stolen buttons, but the real question is why? What was hidden in the box before it was shipped?"

"Or perhaps that's not the issue. It might be a competing dress designer who wouldn't let you have a vintage button collection." He winked. "Don't overthink it. Sometimes, the answer is simply that they wanted them. The excitement of stealing them might have just been a bonus."

"You may be right. After all, you have considerably more experience with the criminal mind than I do." I walked Eddie to the back door. "Have a good shift."

"Thanks—and let your brain rest. Design a new line of gowns. From what Beth told me, you're amazing. Not that I'd know a great design from one at the discount store." He placed his hand on my shoulder, and butterflies fluttered happily in my stomach.

"I have a lot of work to keep me occupied. Dinner was wonderful. Thanks again."

"You can't go wrong with pizza and salad." He stepped onto the deck, taking a moment to appreciate the vast beach from this perspective. "Between you, the inn, and Fiona's place, the views are breathtaking."

Crossing my arms over my midsection to ward off the slight chill in the breeze, I said, "I'm lucky to live here." I focused on Fiona's place, having a clear line of sight to her back entrance. "Eddie, hold up a minute. I'm going to check my cameras to see if we can discover the prankster's identity."

My cell phone was on the kitchen table. I

tapped the app and pulled up the history. Sure enough, ninety minutes earlier, someone wearing a dark maroon hoodie pulled tightly around their face was lugging a window from the alley between the inn and Twice Loved. They leaned the glass against the building, resting it on the step. They looked around and appeared to be waiting for something. Two sharp bangs echoed in the air. They picked up a rock and hurled it at the glass, causing it to shatter, then ran to the beach entrance. "Eddie!"

The door opened and closed. "What did you discover?"

I pressed the replay button and then handed my phone to him. "Check this out."

"This is great information. Can I take a clip and text it to myself?"

"Absolutely. We have the culprit on video." I did a little dance in place. "One step closer."

"Not exactly; I can't tell if this was a man or a woman. However, it implies that they were working together due to the timing of the firecrackers. Unfortunately, once they made it to the beach, they disappeared."

"This doesn't help at all?" I sank into a kitchen chair.

"Every grain of sand is essential for creating a beach, just as every clue brings us one step closer to identifying the perpetrator. On the positive side, we can see that the individual who broke the window is slender, strong enough to carry a window on their own, and a runner."

A flare of hope sprang inside of me. "I'll add these details to my board."

He handed me my cell phone. "It's a good thing you thought to check the footage."

I tilted my head. "Why didn't you ask? You know about the cameras and their angles."

With a grin, he said, "I wanted to give you time to think about what might come next. If you're determined to ferret out clues, it's best to create your own process."

"And what if I hadn't?" I took a screen-shot of the person and sent it to my printer. It was going on the board as well.

"I would have asked before I left."

My eyes narrowed. "You were on your way down the steps when I thought of it."

"Correct. However, I was still here; therefore, I had the opportunity to wait a few more minutes before asking."

"Hmm. Do you enjoy testing me?"

His grin faded. "I want you to stay safe. If you use logical and critical thinking while you examine clues, it will help you."

"Are you condoning my poking around?"

"Not in the least. Acceptance of what you're doing isn't the same as agreeing with it." He bobbed his head. "I gotta go, but I'll check in later, if that's okay."

"Checking to see if I come up with a new idea?"

His hand rested on the doorknob. "Something like that." Looking across the shadow-filled beach, he said, "Be careful."

"I know, the person is out there some-where, and they know I'm involved. Fiona's my friend."

"I get that you want to help her but de-velop the logical side of your brain." He pulled the door closed.

Herman drifted close. "Eddie's a good man."

I sighed. "Don't I know it."

My ghost chuckled. "What's your next step?"

I said, "Update my board and forget about it. Right now, everything is so chaotic that I can't think clearly."

"Talk to me. Tell me what's got you be-fuddled."

I took the printed copy of the screenshot and taped it to the board. "This is our suspect."

Herman floated closer. "It's a woman or a young man, as in teenager."

"How can you tell?" I peered closer.

"Slim hips, delicate hands, and the way

they lean while setting the pane of glass. It's heavy for them, even though they can manage. If a fit man were handling it, it would be less of a struggle."

I could see what he said as he pointed out each feature. "The hood obscures the face."

"As it was meant to do. You can't expect someone who's trying to fly under the radar to reveal their identity."

"Yeah, I know. But it would have been nice if the hood had slipped a little." I jotted down the time of the bangs we heard and when we arrived at Fiona's. "There are so many unknown variables, and it's driving me buggy."

"Eddie had the right idea; put it aside and concentrate on something you want to do. I've often found that when I put a problem aside, the answer comes more quickly than if I had focused solely on it."

I placed the marker on the table. "You're right. I'm going into the shop to work on the attendant dress design to ensure it coordinates with the vintage wedding dress."

"Excellent. I'll join you." He floated through the door, and I shook my head. I'd never get used to how he appeared and disappeared.

When I arrived in the workroom, Herman's transparent form lounged across the worktable. He waved to the small, upholstered chair and ottoman I had placed in the room. "I'm ready if you are."

My sketchbook and drafting pencils were on a shelf next to the chair. I adjusted the floor lamp so that the paper would be well lit. "I'm going to put the gown on my dressmaker's form. It might inspire me."

Herman was quiet while I adjusted the gown. The train extended from the dress, and I could partially visualize the back and the row of missing buttons. I walked around the dress, noting the details of lace, but it was the drape of the neckline and skirt that sparked my creativity.

With long, bold strokes, I sketched an A-line chiffon skirt and examined what I had drawn. "It needs more elegance, don't you think, Herman?"

I held the pad up for him to take a look.

He tipped his head. "Pleat the corset so it drapes into folds down the front. Do you know what the ladies prefer for the bodice: capped sleeves, strapless, or something else?"

"I'll design the dress with different looks, and they can choose. This one will have one shoulder with a ruffle at the neckline." I quickly drew the overarching flow of the dress. When inspiration struck, it often flowed from my mind's eye to the page just as it was doing now. I tore that page off and began another sketch. This time, the top was a halter version with netting providing modesty. The same long sweep of the skirt would be the element that tied the dresses together as a theme.

I tapped the end of the pencil against my lip. What about the MOB-zilla? An A-line lace dress with a sweetheart neckline, flattering for most women. The finishing touch was a drape of chiffon from her hips, allowing the garment to move with her and making the lace play peek-a-boo. Drama and elegance tied together would be just right for Mrs. V.

I tipped my head from side to side as it cracked and popped. "Herman, how long have I been sketching?"

"Time is no longer relevant to me, so I'm not sure." He gestured to the footstool. "If the stack of drawings is any indication, it's been quite a while."

I sorted through them. "There are some pretty good designs here. Not just for the Vanderkemp wedding, but I could also adjust these slightly for other wedding parties."

"Fabrics and lace make a huge difference; the movement of a gown is greatly affected by both."

I frowned.

"Of course you knew that; I was just confirming." His voice faded.

I couldn't help but laugh a little. "Herman, is this what it would have been like if you were still alive, trying to cajole the best from me?"

"It's what mentors do, even in their ghostly form."

I set my book and pencil aside. "Why do you think there aren't any loose threads in the case of Fiona's assault?"

"Are we back on the case, Ms. Sofa Sleuth?"

"Yes. Don't you find it unusual? You've known Fiona for years. Has anyone ever broken into her store before this?"

"Not that I remember." He floated toward me and hovered in midair. "Is that important?"

"Buttons. It's all about those darn buttons, and we may never know what was in that box." I stood up and said, "I'm going for a walk."

"Do you think that's a wise idea? It's late, and after what happened tonight, maybe it'd be best for you to wait until daylight to search for whatever just popped into your head."

"If I'm correct, there could be a clue the police overlooked."

"Like?" Herman hovered in front of me as if his physical presence could stop me from leaving.

"Could the perp have stashed the button box? We know they dropped the cupcake wrapper in the alley. It might have been easier to leave it and go back after it."

"Wouldn't they have already come back?"

I arched an eyebrow. "Maybe that's what the distraction was about tonight: to see if anyone would come flying out to investigate. Right after the incident, the cops were all over that place."

"The trash company picks up in the morning. If they hid the box in the alley, you don't have long to locate it."

"What makes you think I'm focused on the alley?"

"You mentioned the wrapper. If I were you and it were me looking around, I'd be more obvious. In the front and back of Fiona's store are overgrown shrubs mixed in with the annuals she planted. If I were looking to hide a box, that's where I would leave it for safekeeping."

"If I'm not back in…" I paused. "Never mind. There's nothing you can do if I'm not back in an hour."

"Text Beth and tell her what you're doing. When she gets home from her date, she can check in to make sure that your adventure was either successful or a bust."

"Good idea." I quickly typed a message. "Now, dark clothes, a flashlight, and I'm off."

"If you're seen, people will think you're a peeping Thomasina."

"Then I should keep a low profile."

• • •

"Standing motionless outside my back door, I silenced my cell phone. While waiting for my eyes to adjust to the low light, I listened harder than ever. Were those footsteps I heard growing closer? They clicked as if they were high heels. Then, they stopped.

I held my breath, not moving until I knew who those feet belonged to. It seemed like forever, but finally, the steps started again. *Click. Click,* against the cement walk, a slow and steady pace.

I could use the flashlight as a weapon, just in case I needed one. Around the corner between me and the town hall emerged a Great Dane. He paused and sniffed the air before meandering closer. Was the pup alone?

He lumbered closer to me, but no one was behind him. A sharp whistle pierced the night, causing the dog's head to snap in that direction before he trotted off. I exhaled softly; as much as I wanted to laugh, I didn't.

It was just someone walking their dog off-leash. While it might be breaking a rule, that dog wasn't about to hurt anyone. I'd bet he was looking for a Scooby Snack.

Now that my eyes had adjusted to the lighting, I stayed close to the back of my building and the inn as I crept toward the alley, taking care to move as quietly as possible. I tested each footstep for any crackling twigs. Once I reached the alley entrance, the dumpster was fifteen feet away. I clicked on my flashlight and tucked the lens against my coat to control the beam.

I paused and listened, but the air was still. The only sound was my breathing. Reminding myself to stay calm, I crouched down and peered under the metal container. Tucked against a wheel was a shiny oval object. My fingers wrapped around it.

"FREEZE!"

13

I glanced over my shoulder into the bright beam of light. My voice trembled. "Wait."

"Get to your feet, and don't make any fast moves."

The commanding voice behind the light made my stomach drop. "Rhonda. It's Claudia Grant."

"Officer Perkins."

I kept my hands visible to her, even though I was clutching the small object between my thumb and forefinger. I repeated the same movement with both hands to prevent her from asking questions about what I had.

"What are you doing out here?"

"Can you lower the light? It's hard to concentrate when staring into it."

"How can I be sure you don't have a weapon?"

I groaned. "I don't have a gun, a knife, or a candlestick."

"This isn't a game, Claudia. You've been caught trespassing, dressed like a burglar under the cover of darkness. What would you think if you were in my shoes?" The light remained steady. "Never mind. Don't answer that."

I needed to come up with a plausible explanation for why I was rummaging under the dumpster. "I thought I dropped something when I took the trash out."

"This is the Whistler's Inn trash receptacle. Isn't yours behind your store?"

I disliked how she placed unnecessary

emphasis on *your store,* although she wasn't wrong. "I had extra trash today, and Mariah mentioned it would be fine since their dumpster is getting picked up early in the morning."

"If I were to ask her, she'd confirm your story?"

I swallowed the lump in my throat. "Yes."

A police cruiser arrived, its strobing blue lights reflecting off the buildings. The driver's door swung open. "Officer, what's going on?"

A voice I recognized instantly. Eddie.

"I caught Miss Grant skulking around the alley."

"Not skulking. Taking out the trash."

"Claudia, lower your hands, and Perkins, your flashlight?"

I did as he asked, but very slowly, in case Rhonda had a different idea. She turned the light from my eyes, but it continued to illuminate the area.

Eddie crossed the alley to stand between

us. "Claudia, is there any reason you had to take out the trash now? It's kind of late."

"It is, but you know the trash man comes before sunrise, and I wanted to make sure I didn't miss it."

He took in my dark clothes and black sneakers. "Nice outfit." I could hear the teasing in his voice, but I cringed. He had seen me earlier in the evening and knew I had changed.

"Thank you. Dark colors are slimming."

His lips twitched. "Maybe you should head back to your apartment, and next time you take out the trash this late, wear a reflective vest so you're not mistaken for someone else."

"Good tip. Thanks." I hurried past Rhonda, still clutching the prize of the adventure, and jogged up my stairs, glancing at the officers. I was far enough away that I couldn't hear what they were saying, but Rhonda slapped her hand against her thigh. Her frustration was palpable. Eddie caught me watching them and didn't break his stare. I did, so I slipped into my apartment.

I removed the dark ball cap, my hair cascading down my back, and tossed it into the closet. My sneakers rested by the door as I padded in my stocking feet into the living room, switching on a bright lamp before gazing at my treasure.

A pearl. The soft, lustrous sheen of what I guessed to be a 12-mm pearl must be natural, given its irregular shape. Cultured stones have a more perfect form. I wasn't an expert, but I'd seen many pearl buttons during my time at the design house, and this one wasn't just a simple button. However, it was one of the most stunning gems I had ever held. It could have been worth the risk if this fell from the stolen box. I flipped open my laptop and did a quick search. A single non-cultured sea pearl could range from $65 to $ 5,000, whereas a freshwater pearl of the same grade ranges from $400 to $6,000.

Herman drifted into the living room. "How did the sleuthing turn out?"

I held out my hand with the prize nestled in my palm. "I found this near the dumpster before Rhonda Perkins snuck up on me." I narrowed my eyes. "Which is interesting since I never heard a car. What was she doing on foot patrol at that time of night?"

He zipped over to the window. "Since when does local law enforcement conduct foot patrols? Aside from the parking attendant, it's not normal."

"I'll ask Eddie tomorrow. I'm confident he'll want to know what I was doing out there and if I found something."

"What was your defense for being in the alley?" He was floating in mid-air in front of me.

"Taking out the trash. My flimsy excuse was that Mariah gave me permission to dispose of extra trash that wouldn't fit in my bin." I grabbed my phone and sent her a quick text in case Rhonda thought to check my statement.

"Covering your bases, Gigi?"

I looked up through my lashes. "You don't need to call me that."

"I like it." Herman's form drifted from the room. "I'll be in my shop."

I didn't respond. My uncle's poor ghost, caught between this world and heaven, and I felt terrible for him. Once I finished adding the new clue to the board, I would read more in the book *Help Your Friendly Resident Ghost Cross Over*. There had to be something I could do to ease his transition.

I crafted a small pillow from facial tissue and placed the gem in the center before taking photos to post on my board. Satisfied with the little progress I'd made tonight, I smiled. Beth will be excited when she sees the new clue I discovered.

Was the pearl genuine or simply an excellent imitation? I needed to speak with a reputable jeweler to have it evaluated. A trip to

Portland after Julia's fitting tomorrow was now on the agenda. But first, I needed to gather a list of shops to visit. Ideally, if I could find an antique jeweler, they would be able to provide me with more information than someone who could just tell me the value. At least, that was my hope.

I opened a search window on my laptop and typed *best jewelry stores in Portland.* A list of over twenty names appeared. I refined my search to the top five and took a screenshot to send to my phone. As I looked closer, one business caught my attention: R. C. Gavin Antique Jewels. That was the first stop on my list. If I didn't glean anything relevant, I'd move on to the others in town because someone had to know about that stone. "Herman, I'm making progress."

I looked around. That's right, he had done his Houdini act. I ran my hand down Lola's back. "Are you interested, little girl?"

She answered me with a head tilt and a purr. I scratched around her ear. What was

Rhonda doing in the alley? I knew that question kept circulating in my mind, but it still didn't make sense.

I tapped a message to Eddie asking him if there was foot patrol after dark and hit the send button before I could change my mind. Waiting until morning would prevent me from getting a good night's sleep.

As I got up from the sofa, I turned off the living room lights and glanced diagonally across the street at Beth's apartment. Her lights were ablaze, indicating she was not only home but also awake.

I called her cell phone. When she answered, I asked, "Hey, are you alone?"

She laughed. "Yes, we had a good time, but no other details are forthcoming. What's up?"

"Could Ethan cover the shop tomorrow afternoon? I need to take a trip to Portland and thought you might enjoy coming along for the ride."

"Oh?"

I had her undivided attention now. "I have a fitting with Julia at ten, but we'll be done by eleven or noon at the latest."

"That'll work."

I saw her standing at her window, looking in my direction. With a grin, I waved and said, "I found something, and I'll share all the details tomorrow in person. Suffice it to say it was a decent night for the sofa sleuths."

"Dang it. Now I wish I hadn't gone out on a date."

"Don't be ridiculous. Dating is beneficial for the soul. Besides, if Rhonda had found us *both* lurking in the alley, it would have been difficult to explain."

She let out a soft whistle. "Wow, now I can't wait to hear the details."

"I'll tell you everything tomorrow. But did you confirm whether Luke is going with us to the fall festival?"

"He is," she sighed dramatically. "Claudia, I really like this guy."

"That's fantastic. He's dating a great woman, too."

"You have to say that. You're my best friend."

I laughed. "It's the truth, so don't forget it. For tonight, get some rest, and tomorrow wear comfortable shoes. We may do some walking in downtown Portland."

"Sounds like a plan. Would you like to have a late lunch when we get there?"

"Sure. Come over any time after twelve, or if Julia leaves earlier, I'll text."

"Have a great night."

"You too, Beth."

Herman drifted into the darkened room. "Are you and Beth going someplace?"

I picked up the pearl and tucked it into my handbag for safekeeping. I didn't want Lola to use it as a tiny ping-pong ball for her amusement.

"We are. A trip to Portland is the next step in our investigation. I found an antique store that specializes in jewelry. If they can estimate its worth, it will give me a better idea of what else might have been in that cigar box."

"And you're sure this came from that box?"

"Logically speaking, yes. It couldn't have been there long; otherwise, the weight of the dumpster wheels running over it would have ground it to dust."

He bowed his head. "That makes sense. Have you considered the possibility that it might be a fake?"

"Not really. The stone's luster and texture make me believe it's genuine. The only serious question is, what's it worth, and is it worth the risk of going to jail?"

"In a few short hours, you'll know."

I picked up my phone and noticed Eddie had texted back. "Huh. Get this. I texted Eddie about Rhonda's surprise appearance in the alley. He said there are no foot patrols at night unless there is a festival."

I looked at Herman's floating form.

"Now that you have confirmation, your

next question is: What was she doing out there?"

"In uniform." I tapped out thanks and walked into my bedroom.

Herman lingered in the hall, allowing me some privacy as I changed into my pajamas and brushed my teeth before getting into bed. "You can come in, now."

He appeared through the wall. I wished he had entered through the door, but it didn't seem to bother him, and I tried to let it go. It was just his quirk, and I'm sure I had enough of my own that annoyed him.

"Can we talk about that disaster of an old gown?"

I smiled. "It's not a disaster, just not well cared for. There's a difference. If you half-close your eyes and look at it on the dress form, you'll see what it once was, not the yellowed, brittle lace brought to the shop for me to remake."

"It's easy to see you're up for the challenge. Have you ever worked on a gown in this condition before?"

"I had one that was worse. Unfortunately, that dress was a complete remake. I used pieces of lace and fabric as panels and over-lays for a similar design. In the end, the bride was happy." I adjusted my blankets. "What I don't understand is that Mrs. V is fastidious about every detail concerning the wedding. She doesn't seem like the type to have a family heirloom neglected in preservation, so why is this dress in such poor condition?"

"I wondered the same thing. You could ask Julia about the gown's history and, during that time, find out why the gown was left hanging in a closet somewhere. I'd guess it wasn't even in a garment bag."

"True. She brought the dress draped over her arm, not even on a hanger."

"Like it came from a thrift store or something?"

I reflected on Herman's question. "No. As if it weren't special. Yet, if the dress wasn't that important to her, then why does she want to wear it?"

"There are things I can't answer, but you can ask her tomorrow to unearth the secret of the dress."

"You can count on that." I turned off the light and lay back. The comforting darkness filled the room. "Herman, are you sad?" I had intended to read a few pages in the ghost book, but exhaustion washed over me.

"That's an unusual question. As a ghost, I don't experience the full range of emotions like I did when I was flesh and blood. They're muted like a watercolor painting. What makes you think I'm sad?"

"You're stuck with me in the apartment or shop. I know you've tried to slip through the walls to the deck, but it's like hitting a brick wall for you. It must be, at the very least, annoying."

"I get frustrated that I can't pick up a pin, handle fabrics, or demonstrate a technique that is slightly different from what you use. I wanted this time together to be hands on, a passing of the scissors, if you will. It shouldn't be about you dealing with a ghost and trying to figure out the business through a verbal commentary. This isn't how I envisioned passing the business on to you."

"I don't blame you for what happened. If anything, I should have come up sooner. I could have spent my summers here during college absorbing your knowledge instead of returning to my mom's and catching up with my high school friends."

"You were doing what all college kids do, enjoying your last summers without the adult responsibilities you'll have for the rest of your working life. Don't carry any regrets. I'll find a way to teach you everything I can. Who knows, maybe this will be even better. I can certainly pop in and out at any time."

I gazed at my uncle's translucent form, which glowed softly in the moonlight. "You're a kind ghost and uncle."

"Good night, Claudia. Tomorrow is a busy day," he said, fading away.

14

I unlocked the shop's front door five minutes before ten. Julia would be arriving any moment, and I had her dress on the form in the center of the salon. My pin box, sketchpad, and pencil were on a small table nearby. I was prepared to take notes, ask questions, and unearth new information about dresses and buttons.

Beth stood at the doorstep of her shop, hanging her OPEN flag. She turned and waved at me. As I waved back, Julia pulled up alongside the sidewalk, redirecting my attention to her.

"Good morning, Julia."

The passenger door swung open, and Sienna stepped out.

"Hello, Sienna. What a surprise!"

Julia stepped out and gave me a tight smile as Sienna walked behind the car and smoothed the front of her blouse. "Good morning, Claudia. When Julia mentioned she was coming, I thought we could chat about the attendant dresses, too. She said you were going to work up a few ideas."

"The more, the merrier." I held the shop door open as the ladies walked inside. I needed to be circumspect about how I questioned the bride, but this could be an opportunity to discuss the auction.

"You may place your handbags on the side table. I have no other appointments until tomorrow, so you have my complete attention, and the shop is at your disposal. May I offer you a cup of tea or some water?"

"Nothing for me, thank you," Julia said, glancing at Sienna, who shook her head. "We're fine. Thanks, Claudia."

"As you can see, I have the dress on the form. I was hoping we could talk about the condition of the gown."

Julia and Sienna sat on the sofa.

She asked, "What would you like to know?"

I considered how to discuss the condition of the dress. "After meeting your mother, Julia, I'm surprised the gown isn't in better shape; well, that it wasn't protected from elements like dust and sunlight. The brittleness of the lace indicates it was left uncovered for an extended period."

Julia placed a hand over her heart. "It's not my family's gown. It's a Madison wedding dress."

Like a safe with the spin of a turn dial, a tumbler dropped on the lock of this puzzle. "I thought it was from your mother's family."

Sienna said, "All Madison brides wear

something from the family. The dress was important to my brother. We discovered it in a trunk while playing in the attic as kids. When I learned about this shop and your magic with a needle, I thought you could be the designer to give it a new life."

"Do you have any idea what happened to the buttons? Perhaps they're still in the trunk."

She shook her head. "I don't think so."

I waited for several seconds to see if she would expand on her comment. When she didn't say anything else, Julia spoke up. "Tristan remembers his grandmother removing them when she caught them playing dress-up. I can ask him if they know where they might be if you think that would be easier than trying to find replacement buttons."

"The original is always best, as the loops were stitched for the precise size. However, after closely examining this dress, I'm not sure if it's necessary since Julia wants to update the dress and adjust the fit. We might need to use a different type of button."

Sienna stood. "If you're not capable…"

I gestured for her to sit down. "Sienna, I didn't mean to upset you. But the gown is fragile. I can launder it, and with the family's permission, I can use sections of the lace that are in good condition as a bodice or sleeve overlay." I took my sketch pad and drew a rough idea of what had percolated in my mind. "I didn't want to take the liberty of moving forward without a consultation." I crossed the space between us and, sitting on the arm of the sofa, handed Julia the pad.

"As you can see, the drape of the new design is similar to the current gown. I've echoed the modest round neckline, and it's fitted at the waist with pleats cascading down to the slim skirt. However, the back of the dress features a detachable train and an option for bustling, allowing for ease while dancing the night away. I can incorporate the lace on the bodice and cuffs, provided there's enough to extend down the back of the train."

Julia studied the page, her finger trailing down the lines of the front of the dress. "Can we add a row of buttons in the back?"

"Of course. Seed pearls would be lovely." I glanced at Sienna, noticing that her lips pressed together in a thin line.

"It's a beautiful dress, but if you take apart the Madison gown, it will be in pieces when you're finished." Her eyes locked on mine. "Is this the best option?"

"You're free to consult another seamstress, but in my professional opinion, it is."

Herman drifted into the room and hovered near the dress form. "You can tell that snippy woman that fabrics are delicate and must be treated properly."

Julia placed a hand on Sienna's arm. "I want to work with Claudia. If she believes this is the best option and it's important to

Tristan that I wear the family wedding gown, then we should have it remade. This new garment will incorporate both old and new elements, ensuring it remains timeless for generations to come."

"As long as you preserve it, fabrics—especially handmade lace—are subject to degradation over time." I saw Herman nod. "I stitched a toile, a practice dress, that we can modify."

Sienna arched her brow. "Were you planning to dissuade Julia from wearing the gown?"

"Not at all. But in my shop, I have what you could call templates—basic types of dresses that can be utilized to create new designs. Once we have a design and I know exactly where we'll incorporate lace, I'll carefully launder your gown, let it air dry, and then take it apart."

Sienna shuddered. "Will you throw out what you don't use?"

"Not at all. I will package it carefully and

return it to you. Perhaps someday some parts of the gown could be used in an heirloom quilt."

She nodded in agreement. "If you want this new gown, I'll support you."

With a grateful smile, Julia said, "Thank you."

"Madison. I wonder." I tapped my lower lip as I dropped the baited hook to see if Sienna was curious about what occupied my thoughts.

She asked, "What are you thinking, Claudia? Do you have another idea for the gown?"

"Not directly. A box of antique buttons was purchased from an auction by a shop in town, Twice Loved, which is two doors down. Anyway, the shop owner, Fiona, bought several lots from Bucks and Bidding Auction House. They mentioned it came from the Madison family. Was that your family that included several boxes for sale, one of which contained old fabrics and another a cigar box filled with buttons?"

Sienna said, "I don't handle those kinds of events. That would be Tristan. Did you check if any of the boxes had buttons that would suit Julia's dress?"

"Unfortunately, that box was stolen a couple of nights ago."

The color drained from the women's faces.

Julia said, "That's terrible. I hope she wasn't hurt badly."

She didn't specify whether the robbery was worse or if the attack was more distressing. "Luckily, Fiona wasn't seriously injured. The hospital kept her overnight for observation. Unfortunately, she never had a chance to sort through the button box, just a quick glance. I wonder if it might have contained something suitable for this gown?" *Had I mentioned she was attacked? Or did Julia assume?*

"Do the police have any leads on the attacker?" Sienna asked, her face emotionless and mirroring Julia's.

"Not yet. But I'm confident they'll find out who it was and arrest them."

"The shop owner hadn't looked inside the box. I would have unpacked and sorted it out immediately after the box arrived. I'm not the most patient person when it comes to buying items." Sienna clutched her hands in her lap. I wouldn't describe her actions as distress; it felt more like anger.

"All she got was a glance. She purchased the boxes for me since I am passionate about vintage and antique clothing."

"What are the authorities doing to locate it?" Julia hadn't taken her eyes off me. "And attacking an elderly woman," she shook her head, "is just appalling. I'm glad to hear she's doing better."

I crossed my ankles, unsure of what was happening with these ladies. If I let them ramble long enough, would they confess to breaking into the shop? If they did, why? Sienna's family was the one who put the boxes up for auction. "Have you gone into Twice Loved? It's a charming shop if you enjoy collectibles and vintage items."

Sienna replied, "No, we haven't wandered in. The few times we've visited Drakes Bay we haven't had the time. We've been on a tight schedule. Even today, when we leave, we have other commitments."

Was it strange that Julia allowed her future sister-in-law to do all the talking? She didn't seem shy when she was here yesterday.

"Yes, so much to do for the wedding. We're checking several venues." Julia licked her lips. "Busy. Busy."

"How did your search go yesterday?"

Bright pink spots flushed her cheeks. "I had a headache, so I went home. Besides, when I messaged Sienna, she suggested that we do it together. Two heads are better than one."

"Yes. Well," I said as I stood. "Would you

like to try on the toile dress? The practice version of your gown?"

Julia beamed. "Yes. Please."

Now she looked like an excited bride. "If you want to go into the large dressing room, I'll bring it in." I handed Sienna my portfolio. "I've created several sketches of attendant gowns. If you'd like to look, please let me know which ones you prefer. We can get Julia's opinion after her fitting. This way, I can start on Betsy's and your gowns before the next appointment."

With a huff, she took the leather case. "You're not digital?"

I shook my head. "It's not in the preliminary design stages. Once I get closer to the final product, I'll transition to the electronic version." To avoid further questions about my process, I went to my sewing area and slipped the toile off the hanger.

Herman appeared. "This is a great start. I hope the bride can see your vision."

In a whisper, I said, "Me too."

I crossed the salon to the dressing room and knocked on the door. "Julia, are you ready for me to come in?"

The door swung open, revealing her in a slip. Her face glowed as tears welled in her eyes.

"What's wrong?" I set the hanger on a hook and wrapped my arms around her shoulders.

"Nothing." She glanced over my shoulder at Sienna, who was studying the sketches. She lowered her voice. "I can't believe I'm going to be a bride, and we're about to begin work on my gown. Not an old, dusty, itchy version of a dress from a woman I didn't even know existed until a month ago."

"If you didn't want to wear it, why did you agree?" I slipped the muslin over her head.

She wriggled her arms through the sleeves and adjusted the round neckline. "To keep the peace. Tristan and Sienna have a very narrow view of what my dress should be. Right after we got engaged, they started talking about an old, valuable dress in the attic. I just had to wear it. You would have thought it was sewn with pure gold thread or something."

I secured the back with fabric clips. "Now you'll have *your* dress, and it will incorporate the Madison heirloom gown. It will be a perfect blend of old and new—two things off your checklist."

She smiled as she looked in the mirror. "Can you incorporate some of the lace and fabric in my gown without looking frumpy?"

"I give you my word; your gown will be beautiful, and you'll look stunning as you glide down the aisle. Not a single piece of itchy fabric or lace in sight."

"Thank you, Claudia. I'm so glad Sienna discovered your dress shop." Her smile faded. "I wish we had the buttons. Tristan said they were the most exquisite shade of ivory."

I recalled the pearl hidden in my bag. It

was also a lovely shade of ivory. "I didn't realize that he and Sienna had seen the original buttons. I thought you said their grandmother had removed them."

She pressed her hands against the pleats at her waist. "One popped off when Tris and Sienna were playing dress-up. That's when his grandmother took the gown from them. But he never forgot."

"I wonder what happened to the buttons."

She shrugged. "It doesn't matter. I want covered buttons on this dress to hide the zipper."

"Then that's what you shall have." I adjusted the neckline and sleeves until Julia beamed.

Calling over her shoulder, "Sienna, you need to come in here," she swished the skirt from side to side. "What fabric will you choose?"

"I suggest that the attendants wear chiffon dresses. For your gown, let's spice things up a bit. How do you feel about a tulle dress with an illusion back that features lace on the bodice and back? We could adjust the neckline and sleeves to be off-the-shoulder, while still keeping it modest, and add beading in ivory seed pearls to the top and the waistline."

She extended her hand to Sienna and smiled. "That's quite a change! Do you have a drawing?"

"You have stunning collarbones, and the way you hold your head is like that of a princess. We should emphasize your beautiful features." I hurried into the workroom and returned with a different sketch pad—one I reserved for bridal gowns.

"Here you go." I handed her the pad, open to the page with what I hoped would be her gown.

She exhaled. A catch in her voice was evident when she said, "This is my dress."

Sienna squeezed her shoulder. "It's beautiful. I love how you've pulled in the lace. Mixing the old with the new."

"You love it too, Sienna?"

"Tristan's eyes will bug out when he sees you for the first time." She looked at me. "You knew we needed to pivot with the Madison gown before this morning."

I nodded. "Yes, I was hoping you'd agree."

"Thank you. Julia will look stunning; my only regret is the lack of pearl buttons. They would have made a perfect accent."

I didn't want to keep circling back to the buttons, but it was important to understand what had happened to them. It was the reason Fiona was attacked; I just knew it. "Check with your family. Maybe someone knows where they are."

She studied the illustration of the dress. "Someone did, but they're long gone now."

That was an unusual statement. "Don't worry. I can find vintage accessories if that matters to you."

Sienna gave me a long look. "When I get home, I'll check to see if we have any old photos that show them. If you could find something like them, maybe it would work."

My heart rate surged. A picture? Maintaining a steady voice, I smiled. "That would be extremely helpful." Just wait until I tell Beth about this twist.

15

"I'm here." I heard the front door close. Beth strolled into the work-room. "How was the morning?"

"Productive." I slid the tablet across the table. "Julia's wedding dress."

She looked at it. "This is stunning. What about the heirloom?"

"I'm going to use lace and fabric from the original; however, the interesting tidbit about today was the buttons."

Pulling out a stool, she sat at the table. "What do you mean?"

Rubbing my hands together, I grinned. "If the late grandmother Madison is to be believed, the dress was very valuable. However, if we examine the gown, we see that it wasn't taken care of, and the threads left from where the buttons should have been are yellow and dried."

Beth's brow wrinkled. "I'm not following you."

"Hold on." I stood up and set the old gown in front of her. "These cuts aren't recent. The buttons were removed a long time ago, maybe twenty-five years ago. It's hard to say."

"All right, but how does that help us?"

"I'm glad you asked." This time, I withdrew the wad of tissue from my shoulder bag and carefully unfolded it, placing it on the table in front of her. "Last night, I decided to explore the alley after someone broke a window on Fiona's back doorstep."

"What? Is she okay?"

"Sorry, I forgot you didn't know that tidbit. Eddie and I were sharing a pizza when we heard what we thought were a couple of gunshots near the bay. Naturally, we took off running and discovered that someone had placed a window against the door and shattered it, escaping down the shoreline or maybe up. I'm not sure about that part."

Her hand flew to cover her gaping mouth. "Gunshots at the beach?"

"Relax. It was just fireworks, and everyone was fine, well, except for the seagulls. I'm sure they weren't thrilled to have their dinner dive interrupted."

"Claudia, back to the story."

"I'm getting there. Anyway, when I returned to my place, I checked my cameras and said…" I had the footage queued up and handed it to her. "See for yourself."

On the screen, the figure skulked through the back walkway, with the window. "What the heck? Carrying a window and then breaking it. What purpose did that serve?"

"No idea unless it was to see if Fiona

came and flicked the lights on in her apartment. A test to see if she was home?"

"That might be the best possible answer. If I were someone thinking of breaking into a building, I'd want to know if anyone was around."

"Since we live above our shops, they're never truly empty. Are you, Fiona, and I the only ones with owner-occupied apartments?"

"In this part of downtown, yes. Some shops at the southern end of town rent out apartments and have homes elsewhere."

Would I live above the store forever? It was a possibility, yet not something I needed to contemplate today. I pointed to the tissue with the pearl. "Are you curious about where I found that button?"

With a laugh and a smile, she picked it up to examine it. "It's pretty. Is it real?"

"I think so. I discovered it beneath the inn's dumpster next to a wheel. It must have been left behind in someone's rush to escape."

Her eyes widened. "I assume you've re-searched the value of a pearl of this size and shape."

"Of course, which is why we're taking a road trip to Portland. I measured it, and it's roughly 12 millimeters. The shape, depth of color, and luster indicate it's a sea pearl, and if I were the betting kind of gal, it was one of at least a dozen in that cigar box."

Beth folded the tissue and handed it to me. "You should hold on to this," she said as she got up. "Where to first?"

I tucked the tissue-wrapped gem into a zippered pocket of my bag. "I found an an-tique jewelry store in Portland. We should start there. If that doesn't work out, we can try several more stores until we know for cer-tain what we're dealing with."

"What are we waiting for? Let's hit the open road."

"Let me double-check the front door, and then we'll head out the back." I slung my bag over my shoulder and picked up the Jeep keys from the desk. I wanted to let Herman know we were leaving, so I called out to my favorite feline. "Lola, keep an eye on the house and shop. We're going to Portland, and we'll be back in time for your dinner."

Beth smiled. "You've taken a liking to your inherited kitty."

I turned off the overhead lights, and sunlight flooded into the front salon. "What can I say? She's a wonderful companion. I'd be lonely without her."

"That's how Herman felt."

What I couldn't say was if, or rather when, Herman crossed over, there would be a huge hole in my life. Not that I wanted him to stay with me for selfish reasons, but he was my favorite ghost, at least among those I had acknowledged.

The drive to Portland was uneventful—one might say downright dull—except for the trees lining the highway. They displayed colors that I'd love to integrate into my designs. As I slowed down to exit, I handed

Beth my cell phone. "Could you take a few pictures of the trees? The colors are stunning, and if I can incorporate that palette into a fall collection for next year, I believe it would be a big seller."

She took the phone. "Already thinking of next year?"

"Are you kidding? Maintaining a full supply of ready-to-wear and custom designs will keep me working at a breakneck pace for the rest of my career. Unless people grow tired of my designs, then it will be a completely different story."

"You know I've been mulling over an idea and wanted to run it by you. But if you think I'm overstepping or it's a foolish idea, say so. My feelings won't be hurt at all."

With a glance at Beth, I could see the worry lines between her brows. They didn't appear often. "Tell me what's on your mind. I can't say whether it's clever or not until you do."

"Since you mentioned next year's collection, I was curious about your thoughts on including a few knitted pieces. A slouchy sweater paired with trousers, a vest, a dress, or a blanket scarf. I could keep brainstorming ideas."

I playfully slapped her arm. "Are you kidding? Knits are often used to add texture and tone to outfits, not just for fall and winter, but also for spring and summer with cotton yarns. Looser stitches are perfect. Do you want to do the knitting? It's a lot to undertake considering your current workload with the store."

"Not exactly. I'd like to collaborate on the design process, and I can create the patterns. However, a group of people in town are avid knitters. They knit for local craft fairs and hospital bazaars, and they even make baby gift boxes for new moms when they leave the hospital with their babies. If we had some designs, I thought we could hold a meeting to see who would want to knit as a side job. Maybe it would be a limited number of pieces per season. In addition, I could sell the patterns at Knit or Purl."

"Beth, I had no idea you were considering designing. It's a perfect addition to your shop, and I believe this could be beneficial for both of us. What if you create two or three sweaters for the spring line? We could offer one in each size, and if they sell quickly, we can market them as a limited offering but expand for the fall."

She shifted in her seat. "You like the idea?"

I eased off the highway and merged onto the road leading downtown. "I love it. When we get back to Drakes Bay, we should look at what I have planned for the upcoming season, and then you can pick one or two designs and develop a knitted piece to go with it." The GPS announced we were arriving in one mile. "What I like most about this plan is involving others in town and allowing them to not only knit for donations but also benefit financially from their talent."

"I was hoping you'd say that. Some of the older ladies in town might appreciate some extra money."

I parallel parked on the street in front of R. C. Gavin Antique Jewels. We got out, and I looked at the front façade. The display windows contained carefully arranged boxes of rings and watches, and black velvet stands displayed strands of pearls and other precious gems. "This must be the place."

A dancing butterfly fluttered in my stomach. Why was I feeling nervous? This was a fact-finding mission. Either the pearl I had was a convincing fake or something worth stealing. "Ready?"

Beth tilted her head toward the door. "Come on. Let's see what treasure you've found."

The shop brimmed with a variety of antique armoires for jewelry, tabletop jewelry boxes, men's valet stands, dressing tables, and mirrors along one wall. On the opposite wall, glass cases displayed rings, earrings, necklaces, bracelets, and watches. I exhaled. We had found the right place on the first try.

"Hello, may I help you?" A man in his forties approached us. He was tall and thin, sporting a well-trimmed mustache and beard. He wore a pink shirt, dark jeans, a navy-blue sports coat, and black loafers—not what I expected.

"Yes, I'm Claudia Grant, and this is Beth Stewart. We found a pearl and were hoping you could give us an estimate of its value. I believe it's a sea pearl."

"I'm Gavin, and I'm happy to help." He gestured to the counter and picked up the loupe resting on a velvet pad. "Where did you find this gemstone?"

There wasn't an easy way to explain that I found it under a dumpster while searching for clues about a burglary. "It was mixed in with a box of buttons." At least that sounded more believable. "I'm a dress designer, and I sometimes use vintage lace and notions. When I came across this one, I was intrigued by its size and color. It appears to have been drilled in the center, so I'm assuming it was used as a button."

Gavin nodded and turned the stone over, examining it from every angle in the light. His facial expression remained unchanged. Beth glanced at me from the corner of her eye. I shrugged slightly but stayed silent.

He set the pearl on a black velvet tray. "Where did you say you found this?"

"In a box of old buttons?" My voice rose higher as I spoke, and I hated that it sounded like a question. But he wouldn't have asked me again if it was a cheap imitation, would he?

"This sea pearl is of exceptional quality. One that I'd expect to find on a necklace, not used as a button."

"So, is it worth a couple of hundred dollars?"

His gaze bore into mine. "No. In my expert opinion, it is worth approximately four, maybe five thousand."

I gulped and clutched Beth's arm. "Dollars? For a single gem?"

"Yes. Were there more in the box? Even if they were smaller or a different size, they would still be quite valuable. I'd be happy to appraise them for you."

Beth said, "Claudia will check over the box contents again, and if we find more, we'll be sure to return."

Handing me his business card, he said, "If you'd like to sell it, I'd be happy to offer you a fair price. If you're uncertain, I can provide many references who would vouch for my honesty in business." He slipped the pearl into a small velvet drawstring pouch and handed it to me. I secured it in the zipper pocket once more.

An older woman floated into the room. Oh, dang, not another ghost lingering around a business. When I nodded my head, she glided closer.

"Can you see me?"

"Gavin, did your mother or grandmother work here?"

"No, it was my Aunt Minnie's business. I took it over after graduating from college. Unfortunately, she passed away a couple of years ago. Why do you ask?"

"The store has a sense of longevity."

"Well done, young lady. For your peace of mind, Gavin is knowledgeable and under-stands his gems. You can trust him."

A character reference from a ghost was a first for me. I extended my hand. "Thank you for your time; it was a pleasure meeting you." I directed this more toward Aunt Minnie's ghost.

"Come back again. I've never had anyone who could see me before." She floated beside Beth and me as we left.

I took one last look as she waved. Uncle Herman would be proud that I had con-nected with another ghost. How many older shop owners linger after their deaths? Can they all oversee their businesses from here to their final resting place?

"Where to next?" Beth asked.

I unlocked the Jeep and got behind the wheel. "Do you think it's worth getting another opinion? Gavin seemed certain, even wanting to purchase the gem."

"Since you're not looking to sell it but only want confirmation that it might have come from the cigar box, I think we have our answer. There's no way an expensive pearl would have been accidentally dropped in that alley, as no one has been scouring the ground looking for it."

I nodded in agreement. "All right. We assume this pearl was from the Madison family and somehow auctioned along with a box of buttons. Also, Tristan and Sienna's grandmother mentioned they couldn't play dress-up since the gown was valuable. Do you think I'm overreaching if I suggest she cut off the pearl buttons, stashed them in a box, and forgot about them? Only to have someone discover they had been auctioned by accident?"

"If that's how it happened, why not simply ask Fiona for it back? Even if they claimed it was for sentimental value and never disclosed the truth, she's a reasonable woman and would have given it to them."

"And why not say something now, like that stolen box belonged to my family, and here's what was inside? Motive is key to solving the crime."

"Claudia, you're thinking like someone innocent. If you were guilty, you'd never confess to what was in the box—certainly not that it contained precious gems."

My hands tightened around the steering wheel. "Sienna has to be the guilty one; she has a slim build. It could have been her carrying the window." I stared out the windshield "But who is her accomplice? Julia?"

16

———

eth and I drove back to the highway as I contemplated who could have been Fiona's assailant. "Let's say Sienna stole the box, and Julia was her accomplice. Why would she bring the dress to my shop to update it for her wedding and have me search for replacement buttons? All that does is draw attention to the issue."

"People who aren't good at subterfuge?"

I laughed. "An excellent assessment. There has to be more than what we're seeing. Should we stop at Fiona's and ask if we can search the other boxes? I know one had fabric, another had old gloves and hats, and the final box contained costume jewelry." I snapped my fingers. "Could that be a new target? Maybe there are real gemstones stuck in that box, too. That's why Sienna broke the window to check if Fiona was home. Since the attacker had already sent her to the hospital once, she didn't want to do it again."

"Where could Fiona have been last night if not at home? I'm sure she left the lights on in the apartment."

"The back lights were off when we arrived. However, she also didn't react to the fireworks."

"If you and Eddie hadn't gone over there, it could have been a repeat of Sunday."

I merged into heavy traffic. "The ladies seemed upset that Fiona went to the hospital. You know, I just remembered Sienna mentioning she was going to look for a photo of the dress with the buttons intact. Do you think it would be suspicious if I texted her to ask if she's found anything yet?" I glanced at the clock on the dash. "They left a few hours ago—plenty of time to get back to New Castle. I could say I'm going to Twice Loved to see if I can find anything suitable."

Beth smiled. "I appreciate how your mind operates. Would you like me to send the text from your phone?"

"Please. Texting and driving never mix."

I gave her my password, and she asked, "What do you want to say?"

I spoke slowly so Beth could type. "Hi, Sienna. You mentioned you might have a photo of your grandmother's wedding dress. I'm stepping out to see if I can find any buttons at Twice Loved. The owner said she found another box that might contain something suitable for Julia's gown. If you find the picture, could you text it to me? Thanks." I looked at her. "Is that too wordy?"

"I don't think so. You needed to hit all the high points, and that covered it. If you're good, I'll hit send."

I nodded. A whoosh sound slipped out. "What's next?"

"Let's stop dwelling on this case and brainstorm our business venture!" My mood lifted considerably. "How many sweaters would you like to showcase for spring? For reference, I'll have between ten and fifteen originals alongside some staples from Uncle Herman's ready-to-wear dress collection. Those items are classics and never go out of style."

"I hadn't gotten past the part in my head where you say you'd think about the idea. I never expected you to say yes right away."

"Why would you think I'd say no? I'm a fan of your knitwear. I absolutely love the hat and scarf you made for me when I arrived in town."

She waved her hand. "Those were nothing special, just a quick knit and purl edition. I didn't use any cable stitches or fun yarns."

"Classics endure for a reason. In fact, if

you'd like to have some stylish winter sets including scarves, hats, and gloves or mittens for holiday gifts, I'd be happy to put some out for sale."

"I can include those on my list for next year."

"What about this year? We can assess the shoppers' excitement, which could help us determine what to include for the upcoming seasons. That is, if you have time to put together a few sets."

"I can do that! Dad will love this new project, too. As soon as I talk to him, I'll let you know how many gift boxes we can make. I'm thinking ten—unless you think that's too many?" She was speaking so quickly that I wondered how she'd catch her breath.

"Beth, relax. This is going to be fun. I'll also promote it on social media, sharing pictures to showcase what I'll have in stock for the holiday. I have no idea what to expect for sales."

"I'll do the same. Herman used to sell quite a few gift cards during the holidays."

I nodded. "That's good to know." I needed to remind myself to ask Herman what he did for party dresses and when it might get busy. I had found a few items in storage from last season that I could put out; due to his untimely demise, Herman didn't get the chance. These dresses were meant to showcase the season; now they carry a bitter-sweet reminder that he won't be a part of the shopping season.

"Beth, I have some unsold party dresses that Herman made last year. Do you think customers would find it morbid if I displayed them as part of his final creations?"

"His loyal customers would love it." She placed her hand on the console between us. "He'd be proud of you. What you have done with the shop, helping Fiona, and being a good neighbor and friend to me."

"Thanks, but this is the only person I know how to be." I couldn't look at her for fear of getting teary eyed. "I've asked my grandmother and mom to come up for Thanksgiving. I'm not sure what you and Ethan do, but would you like to join us? They're eager to meet both of you."

"I'll speak for Dad. We'd love to join you for Turkey Day." She tipped her head. "Do you cook turkey? Over the past few months, I've seen what I believe is the extent of your cooking skills."

I laughed. "A turkey dinner complete with all the side dishes is one thing my grandmother made sure I could prepare. However, I can't make dessert, so I'll just order those."

"Nope, I've got dessert covered. Dad will bring the wine."

My cell pinged. "Can you see who that is? Maybe it's Sienna."

She confirmed the passcode and then scanned the message. "She says they found one picture, but it's unclear." The phone pinged again. "Oh, she's correct. Maybe if we view it on a larger screen, we can get a closer look."

She held up the phone, but I couldn't focus on the small screen between driving and traffic.

"When I zoom in on the image, the buttons appear round and pearl-like."

"Beth, what if I have tunnel vision?"

"Regarding?"

"These buttons. What if the buttons that were cut off the gown were standard pearl buttons made from mussel shells, and the pearl I found was from a necklace? I mean, who would take high-quality gems and use them as buttons on a wedding dress?"

"It's easy to lose a button, and you might be onto something. I wouldn't use a rare pearl as a button. Heck, I'd be nervous to wear it even as part of a necklace. Can you imagine? I'm not sure how many are on a necklace. If there were fifty, which is a conservative estimate, that's twenty grand hanging around your neck."

I laughed. "Do your math again. It's two hundred grand."

"That's even worse. It's a lot of Jeeps, that's for sure."

I mulled over what we could do next in trying to locate other stones. "We should drop by Fiona's and see if we can get a closer look at the other boxes. Then, we need to study the pictures from the auction house again. There has to be something we're missing."

"I'll call Fiona and see if we can stop by when we get back to town."

"Good. We'll bring coffee and sweets so she can take a break and chat while we look around. Unless, of course, the store is busy."

Beth had the phone to her ear. "It's ringing." She put it on speakerphone.

"Twice Loved." Fiona's voice was strong, and her words were steady.

"Hi, Fiona. It's Beth and Claudia. We were wondering if it would be okay for us to swing by your place and take another look at those boxes you purchased from the auction."

"You can come now if you'd like; I haven't had a customer since before lunch."

"We're on our way back from Portland and should arrive in about fifteen minutes. We thought we'd bring coffee."

"I'm already looking forward to it, and I'll take the boxes down from the shelf for you."

"We can do that."

"Nonsense. Just because I was conked on the head doesn't mean I can't do things. I'm not ancient, you know."

I grinned. She was a ticket, as Herman said. "We just don't want you to overdo it; a head injury is nothing to ignore."

"That was days ago. Come along; I'll be waiting." She disconnected.

Beth said, "I want to be a tough older woman when I am her age."

"Me too. Should I tell Eddie about the pearl and its value? It will be relevant to his case."

"We don't know that for certain."

"Beth, don't you think it's tied to the theft? And don't you suspect Julia and Sienna are involved? And didn't we promise to keep him in the loop as we investigated?"

"That's a lot of ands." She held her phone up. "Do you want me to call him and see if he'll meet us at your place later?"

"What about Rhonda? Should we include her?"

"Knowing her, she will suddenly appear in the middle of your living room while we discuss the news."

"I'll ask Eddie if she needs to come, too." Using my voice command, I instructed my phone to call Eddie, leaving it on speaker so Beth could listen to both sides of the conversation. He answered on the fourth ring. "Hi, Eddie."

"Hey, Gigi. What are you doing? It sounds like you're on the road."

I shook my head. Does he always have to be highly attuned to every background sound? "Driving back from Portland with Beth."

"That sounds fun. Did you ladies close up shop for a midweek adventure?"

"That's why I'm calling. I went to an antique jeweler in Portland."

"Why?"

Now that I had his full attention, I needed to push forward. "Do you remember last night when Rhonda found me in the alley?"

"Yes."

These one-word answers grated on my nerves. "Well, I wasn't taking out my trash."

"What were you doing?"

"I started to think about the person who took the cigar box and the cupcake liner. What if when they cut through the alley, the box opened, and the contents spilled onto the ground?"

"Highly unlikely. Right?"

"Maybe not?" came out as a squeak.

"Gigi, what did you find in the alley? It

better not be anything other than broken glass and empty cans."

I didn't say a word.

"Beth, do you know what she found?"

"I do, but I won't tell you. Claudia is calling you with important information, and you're treating her like a hostile witness in an interrogation when she's on your side."

He sighed heavily.

"Eddie, come over tonight, and I'll explain everything. If you feel it's important to include Rhonda, you can ask her to join us."

"Given her feelings toward you, she'd likely charge you with obstruction of justice or hindering an investigation. I'll take your advice into account and determine how to keep you in the frying pan rather than throw you into the fire."

I gave Beth a high-five smack and grinned. "Great."

"When are you back?"

"We're bringing Fiona a coffee, and we'll

chat for a bit. I think we'll leave her place in about an hour."

"Please tell me you're not going to ask her questions she shouldn't answer, much less even know about."

"She's our friend, and we're concerned about her recovery. You know, ensuring she's not trying to do too much too quickly. Besides, I plan to take her to get the stitches removed, and I want to mark it on my calendar. I'm sure she's scheduled a follow-up appointment." Dang, did he have to see through my motives as if they were plastic wrap?

"You're a good friend. Now, do me a favor while you're there?"

"Sure." I sat up straighter in the driver's seat.

"Please refrain from asking her any questions regarding last night, the firecracker person, or the vandalism on her back step. We, meaning the police department, are currently investigating. I want to avoid upsetting her, as she was unaware of the events."

I didn't want to fib and agree to something I wasn't sure I could avoid. "I would never upset Fiona. She's sweet and needs us to rally around her, helping her feel secure in her home and business."

"I'm glad we're on the same page. However, if you want to urge her to install more cameras, I can support that conversation."

I chuckled. "So, you'll use my influence when it's convenient for you, but you don't want me asking more relevant questions where she might share important clues with me. You know that cops can intimidate the average citizen."

"You caught me. I'm not above using your persuasive techniques if it keeps you safe and off a criminal's radar. Whatever happened to you being a sleuth from the comfort of your living room?"

"Eddie, you know as well as I do that sometimes, during an investigation, you need to get out into the world and ask many questions of experts and potential suspects. I promise to tell you about my two leading suspects and some new evidence tonight. Who knows, I might even stumble across a new clue before I see you."

Beth laughed so hard that her body shook, her hand firmly covering her mouth. She waved at me, leading me to assume she wanted me to wrap up the conversation.

"Can we meet at my place around four?"

"Invite Ethan to join us. He may have an interesting perspective on the two of you meddling in an ongoing investigation."

"We're not just concerned citizens; we're good members of the business community."

"Gigi." That one word carried a distinct warning tone.

"Eddie," I fired back, using the same tone. "We won't do anything to intrude on your job. Try not to worry. We've got this, and we'll be fine."

He said, "Famous last words."

17

───────

*E*ntering Fiona's was always a delight. I inhaled deeply. The shop had the scent of lemon furniture polish, cedar, and leather, along with a hint of mothballs and aged paper. Beth closed the door as I called, "Fiona. We're here."

A muffled response drifted to us. "I'm in the storeroom. Come on back."

We weaved around boxes of what I assumed were new inventory and pushed open the half-closed storeroom door. "Fiona, it's time for a break." I held up the cardboard tray containing three cups of coffee, and Beth waved the white waxed bag in the air.

"I was digging through the last unopened boxes, searching for anything useful for the gown you're working on." She brushed aside a stray lock of gray-streaked hair. Taking a sip of coffee, she smiled. "This will hit the spot. Let's head into the shop; I've set up a small table near the front. I arranged several boxes for you to sort through."

"Do I need to take any of these boxes with us?" I gestured toward the stack of three closest to her.

"We can put those aside for now. They're not from the auction, and I'm not certain what's in them except that I labeled them doodads." She lifted her shoulder and smiled again. "It's my system."

"We all need one." I closed the door as we left the storage space.

Beth said, "You should have seen my system before Dad took over the inventory. I'm not a great organizer, but all his years on the police force helped him become meticulous."

Fiona pulled out a chair near the boxes and then sat in the one next to it. "For you."

Beth took out scones and butter pats from the bag. "All they had left was cinnamon scones; I hope that's okay."

Fiona said, "Any scone is a good scone in my book."

I opened the first box. "Are these from the auction?"

"Yes. Have you learned anything about the items I've purchased?"

I nodded. "This lot came from an estate belonging to the Madison family. In a quirky coincidence, it's the same family that the bride I'm currently working with is marrying into."

Her brow cocked. "That's interesting."

"Isn't it?" I pulled out each piece of folded fabric and gently shook it before refolding it and creating a stack on my chair. So far, nothing had fallen out except for a stray thread or two.

"Do you want help?" Beth asked.

"No, thank you. Enjoy your scone." I sipped my coffee and repeated the same process for the two bundles of lace. As I shook one piece, it felt heavy. I examined it closely and was surprised to find a cameo brooch attached. I unpinned it and handed it to Fiona. "Look at that. It's a bonus."

She turned it over. "It's beautiful. The nose is straight. It could be from the Victorian era."

"The nose is a clue?" I held out my hand to see what Fiona was referring to.

"Absolutely. A tiny nose suggests it was created in the twenty-first century, which is quite common in stores like mine. A strong Roman nose dates back to before 1860. I've only encountered those in museums."

"There's so much to learn about old things." I moved on to the next box, which contained winter gloves and hats. There wasn't anything of interest inside, and some items were moth-eaten. After setting aside the ones in poor condition, I refilled the box with items that Fiona could sell. The final box must contain the costume jewelry. My heart rate quickened as I hoped to find a new clue about what might have been in the button box. If the sea pearl had been there, where were the rest?

Before I opened it, I placed the fabrics in a box to focus entirely on the final container. "I'm going to take these back to storage. Do you want me to throw these away?" I indicated the damaged ones and asked, "In the garbage can?"

"That would be helpful. Thank you, Claudia."

I was back in a jiff.

"Scone?" Beth handed me a paper napkin with a scone. "The box won't go anywhere, and taking your time will help you sort through what's inside."

She knew what I was hoping to find: more

pearls. I glanced longingly at the box before biting into the buttery biscuit.

"What else did you discover from the auction house?"

"Aside from the family's name, nothing. I asked Sienna Madison about the items, and she dismissed it, saying that someone else in her family handled it and she had no idea what had been sold."

"Do you believe her?" Fiona sipped her coffee.

I had no reason to believe she wasn't being completely forthright. Did it matter that my gut told me she was skirting the truth? "Well…"

Beth could see I was hesitating to share my thoughts. She said, "Until the culprit is caught, there's no way to tell who has been honest about the events."

I could now avoid telling Fiona what I thought. "Agreed. The police will catch whoever is responsible."

"I'm glad the two of you think so. I called and spoke to Rhonda—what's her name? That new police officer said there were no new leads. That tells me they've got bupkis."

They would after tonight. Wiping my fingers on the napkin, I wriggled my brows. "I can't resist for another minute. I need to see what's in this box." I looked between Beth and Fiona. "Is anyone else curious?"

Beth raised her hand and smiled. "Me."

Fiona laughed. "I guess you've waited long enough."

I felt like a kid preparing to open a birthday present. I folded back the top, revealing a smaller box inside. I pushed my coffee aside on the table and placed the smaller box in front of me. It felt as heavy as a five-pound bag of potatoes. Lifting the lid, I held my breath—a chaotic, tangled mess awaited me. From the top of the pile, I picked up a pink rose brooch with a seed pearl in the center. It didn't match the sea pearl I found.

"Is this enamel?" I asked, passing it to Fiona, who turned it over.

"It's not that old—maybe forty years. At the time, people used to have jewelry parties, and judging by the signature on the back of the stem, it was a pretty piece but of no value."

Next, there was a vintage ladies' quartz watch. "I'll hand you the pieces as I remove them."

"I'd like to sort as we go. Beth, could you please grab two plastic bins from behind the counter?"

She got up and returned with two shoe-box-sized bins, setting them on the table in the space Fiona had cleared. She dropped the pin and watch into the other bin.

I withdrew several bags of glass bead earrings along with another bag containing more glass beads, including a cuff bracelet. As I pushed aside a copper bangle and several chandelier and clip-on earrings, my mouth went dry upon discovering loose stones at the bottom. I glanced at Beth, trying to convey with my eyes what I was seeing.

Her eyes widened. "Are those what I think they are?"

I picked up an elliptical stone, its luster resembling that of a sea pearl. I selected several more and arranged them on the table. With each gemstone, my heart raced a little faster.

Shifting items in the box, I picked out eleven more, all similar in size and shape.

"Are there any others?"

Fiona was watching me closely. "Claudia, what are those?"

"I'm not certain." I continued to move things in the bottom of the box. I was afraid I'd miss a couple. "Can I use the shoe boxes to transfer the jewelry? I want to make sure we've got all the pearls."

She had a catch in her voice as she asked, "You think they're real, don't you?"

"There's a good possibility they are, and I think whoever stole the cigar box was looking for these. They're from the same lot at the auction."

Fiona got up, rushed to the front door, flipped the sign to CLOSED, and secured the deadbolt. "We don't need any unexpected customers."

I quickly sorted the box. When I finished, there were another eight stones around the same size and color. "We might be looking at a partial necklace."

Clasping her hands, Fiona said, "I need to contact the auctioneer and let him know there must be a mistake."

I took her hands in mine. "We should wait to find out if they're genuine or just an excellent imitation. I know a man in Portland who can appraise them for us, and Fiona, since you bought the boxes, whatever is in them belongs to you."

"However, if it was a mistake, the family should have them returned."

"That's sweet, but you should gather all the facts before contacting anyone," Beth said. "For now, can Claudia take the stones and have them evaluated?"

"And we shouldn't tell anyone what we found until we know for sure." I'd need to explain this to Eddie when I shared the gemstone I'd discovered near the dumpster and its value. He'd be upset if I didn't tell him everything. Additionally, he might know whether they could challenge Fiona's claim of ownership I considered what this could mean for her; it would supplement her retirement savings.

"Not even the police?" Fiona looked at Beth. "What about your father? He'd know what I should do."

"Fiona, I believe we should have the stones evaluated by a reputable jeweler. Once we determine whether they are good fakes or valuable, we can speak with Ethan, who may suggest that you consult a lawyer. That should give us enough time if you could wait until tomorrow."

Her brow furrowed as she picked up several stones and turned them over in her hands. "I'm not an expert, but judging by the feel, these aren't smooth. They have a slight grittiness to them." She handed one to Beth and me. "Feel."

She was right. They were as smooth as silk. "Do you have a small bag I can put these in?"

Pushing back her chair, she strode to the counter, withdrew a small, zippered bag from the shelf, and returned to the table. "Will this do?"

"Perfect." I opened the bag, carefully added the pearls, and closed it. "I'm taking these." I wanted to be crystal clear. We knew what we had found by the serious look on our faces. At least I could tell by the sparkle in Beth's eyes that she and I were on the same page.

"Do what you believe is best. If only the

person had checked all the boxes, we would never have found these."

I thought the same thing. "Let's enjoy our coffee."

The silence wrapped around us. I let my thoughts tumble around with what I knew about the case so far. Nothing made sense. Surely, the ladies, Julia and Sienna, wouldn't have broken into this store and hit Fiona. All they needed to do was ask to see the box and explain there was a misunderstanding about the items that went to auction. In the worst case, they'd have to buy back the boxes for what Fiona paid or maybe for a profit. It was better than risking jail for theft. No one would ever have known the gemstones were inside.

"Fiona, is it your routine to hold off on unpacking boxes when you buy something from an auction?"

"Often, I'm busy when a shipment arrives, so it might sit on the shelf for a week or more. With this purchase, I wanted you to see the buttons."

"Have any other customers come to ask about vintage buttons since the auction?"

"As a matter of fact, yes, a charming older man came in last week—he complimented me on the variety of items I had in the shop. We chatted, and he asked whether I had ever received vintage buttons and jewelry. Many times, people come in looking for specific items, mostly collectors. I mentioned that I had just received several boxes and would unpack them in a couple of weeks. He left me his number, asking if he could have first refusal on the items."

"Is that uncommon?"

"Not really." She put the lid on her cup and placed it in the paper holder. "Would you like to see his card? I believe he has a shop somewhere in New Hampshire."

"Did you call him?"

"No. I wanted you to take what you wanted first, and then I'd give him a call.

There's no reason for him to know I was playing favorites with you."

I smiled, knowing that Fiona's spunk remained intact despite the situation. "Thank you."

"Anything for you. Now it's time to tidy up these boxes and reopen the store. You never know; the next person to walk through the door might just be the biggest sale of the week."

I picked up the boxes and carried them into the storage room while Beth cleaned the table. When I came out, Fiona was standing next to the cash register.

She gave me a business card. "Here's the information for that man."

I scanned it. "Vintage Chic. I've never heard of it." Flipping the card over, I saw a phone number and an address. I pulled out my cell and took a picture before returning it to Fiona. "Did no one else come around?"

"No, just Teddy."

Another tidbit. "Did you get a last name?"

"I never asked. Since I had his phone number, I didn't ask many questions, which isn't unusual either. If I don't know a dealer, they may or may not share their personal information, but most introduce themselves by their first name. It makes the exchange more pleasant."

"Could you please do me a favor?"

"Certainly."

"If Teddy calls to ask whether you've unpacked those boxes, could you mention that you've been under the weather and haven't had the time? However, you'd be glad to call him when you do."

"I don't like to lie."

"Technically, it's not. You were injured, and I unpacked the last of the containers."

She smiled. "True. You're so clever. However, I had told him I'd call."

"Okay, and can you describe his build?"

"He was very tall with broad shoulders, short gray hair cut almost too short, and a long bulbous nose. I believe his eyes were hazel, though I'm not certain about the color. The rest is accurate."

"Wow. I didn't know you had an eye for people."

She shrugged. "Unfortunately, in this business, I must pay close attention to the customers in my shop due to the possibility of shoplifting. A clear description of the person is essential for apprehending them."

"I'm sorry you have to face that un-pleasant reality."

"It doesn't occur frequently, but I'm al-ways ready."

"You know, having a few strategically placed cameras in the shop means that if something happens, the police will have solid evidence to present in court."

"That's why I've decided to install them on the interior *and* exterior doors. Would you remind Eddie the work starts on Thursday?"

On impulse, I embraced her. "Absolutely. I'll come by tomorrow with an update on the pearls."

"I appreciate both of you." She unlocked the front door. "Have a good rest of your day."

"You, too."

Beth and I left the store. "Let's head to my place. Eddie will be there soon, and we have things to discuss."

18

I dashed up the back stairs to my apartment with Beth right behind me. As soon as we entered and closed the door, I squealed.

"Can you believe what we found? Nineteen more pearls. If they are as valuable as the first, that's a lot of cash."

Beth flopped onto the sofa. "What a day. And that man coming into the shop looking for buttons? That's a conversation starter."

"The first thing I want to do is take that

apart. Well, after I hide the pearls," I said, scanning the room. "But where?"

Herman drifted in. "The hidey hole in the pantry cabinet floor is perfect."

I snapped my fingers. "I'll be right back." I gave his ghostly form a wink as I hurried into the kitchen and knelt in front of the pantry. Pushing aside the cleaners, I found the loose board and lifted it, stashing the plastic bag inside. Then I rearranged the bottles and brushed my hands on my pants.

"Would you like something to drink?" I called to Beth.

"Sounds good."

I poured two large glasses of iced tea and added sliced lemon. When I returned to the living room, Beth had the whiteboard out. I felt a wave of relief she hadn't added the newest discovery to it.

"Here you go." I took a seat across from her. "We've had quite the day."

"Ya think? Expensive pearls are popping

up in unexpected places, a New Hampshire mystery man searching for buttons."

I took my laptop from the side table. "Which is the first item we're checking on. The store?"

She nodded.

I typed in the name and New Hampshire, with zero results. I reversed the title from the card, and still, nothing. Next, I called the number, and it went to voicemail. I hung up without leaving a message.

"Zilch?"

I frowned. "The phone number went to voicemail, the electronic kind that says the person you're trying to reach isn't available. Leave a message. There are lots of stores in New Hampshire that use the words chic and vintage in their store titles, but nothing like what's on the card."

"A dead end. Interesting."

I got up and wrote on the board: *Teddy, button man, NH*. Then I added *genuine pearl* and *dumpster*.

"Will you tell Eddie about the pearl and Teddy?"

"Yes, to both. He can track down the phone number, which may or may not lead to Teddy, and he should know about the pearl and where I found it. It must have come from that cigar box after the thief crept out of Fiona's apartment."

With a sharp nod, she said, "I'm glad you're sharing almost everything with him. I know it seems like there's no movement on the case, but Eddie wouldn't let anyone in this town get hurt, nor would he try to *not* solve the issue. It's just how he's wired."

"Good to know. I'm uncertain about Rhonda. Her obvious dislike of me suggests that she thinks I'm guilty of something, or I'm not sure what else it could be."

Beth laughed. "You're joking! She thinks you and Eddie are an item." She added air quotes around *item* before continuing, "He took your side in the alley incident and supported you being with Fiona the night of the attack. From her perspective, he's unavailable for her to date."

"Why would you want to date a co-worker? That gets messy."

"From what I've heard, that's what she did at her last department, which is why she left."

"If that's why she's taken an instant dislike to me, she's off base. Eddie and I are friends. Nothing more."

She flashed me a smug grin. "Your favorite cop will be arriving soon. Is there anything else we should discuss before he gets here?"

A sharp rap on the door interrupted our conversation. "There he is now." I crossed the room and waved him in.

He wore his uniform, causing my pulse to race. Eddie was a good-looking man, and if circumstances had been different, maybe we could have dated. Now, I found myself in the friend zone, so that wouldn't happen.

"Hey. I'm going on shift in a half hour."

"I guessed with the uniform and all." Inwardly, I sighed. "Come on in. Would you like something to drink?"

"No, thanks." He saw his cousin when he entered the living room. "Hey, Beth."

"You don't seem thrilled to see me," she smiled. "But then again, considering how busy we've been today with your case, I understand why."

"At least you agree it's a police matter."

I walked behind him and stood beside the board. "As promised, I'm going to update you on what we've discovered today."

Beth looked at me, her mouth agape. I gave her a wink.

He crossed his muscular arms over his chest. "I can hardly wait."

"Don't be fresh. We know you don't like us meddling, but what we've uncovered is really, really good stuff. And don't worry. I didn't ask Fiona anything I shouldn't have."

He tipped his head. "Did you get an update on the cameras?"

"Yes. Not only is she installing exterior cameras, but she's also getting them placed inside the shop. I believe the events of the past few days spooked her."

"Well, at least something good came out of it." He gestured to the board. "Have you added any of your juicy tidbits?"

"I have. Starting with the reason we went to Portland earlier."

"That was curious."

His stare was intense, and I felt color rising in my cheeks. Clearing my throat, I said, "I wanted to see an antique dealer that specialized in gemstones because last night when I said I was taking out the trash..."

He snorted. "I didn't buy that excuse."

I narrowed my eyes. "That was for Rhonda's benefit and we've already covered that topic previously. Now, stop and listen with both ears. This will ramp up your investigation."

"How so?"

His short questions drove me up the wall,

but I needed to get used to them since we had less than thirty minutes to discuss all the details. "As I was saying, when I looked around the dumpster, something caught my eye underneath it." I didn't need to mention that I was deliberately looking under it.

"You found something important?"

I withdrew the black velvet pouch from my shoulder bag. "Hold out your hand."

Eddie did as I asked, and I placed the pearl into his cupped palm. "I found this."

He rolled it around in his hand. "It's a fake pearl. It could have been dropped there at any time. I don't see how this is relevant to the case."

A smile filled my face. "That's where you're wrong. It's not fake. It happens to be a sea pearl worth four to five thousand dollars. In my opinion, that wasn't just tossed aside. Whoever dropped it will probably come back and look for it."

"Holy cow! Are you sure about its value?" He took the bag, placed it back inside, and tucked the pouch into his chest pocket. "Evidence."

"I thought you might take it," I said, handing him Gavin's card. "You can reach out to this dealer if you need confirmation."

"Good work, but you should have handed the stone over to me or Rhonda last night. Withholding evidence can be misinterpreted by a new, overly eager police officer." He took a picture of the business card and handed it back to me.

"She was not in the mood to listen to me, and at that time, I had no idea if it was anything important. If it were fake, it wouldn't have brought me any closer to Fiona's attacker."

"Bring you closer to the perp. Isn't that *my* job?"

I swallowed the lump in my throat. My chin quivered. "Can you look at this that I saved you valuable time?"

He nodded because I had good intentions. "What else have you found?"

"You should investigate alibis for Sienna Madison and Julia Vanderkemp. They have a similar build to the individual in my security camera footage."

"And these women are?"

"My new clients brought in the Madison wedding dress for me to revamp; they are the same family that auctioned off those four boxes Fiona purchased. When I asked Sienna about them, she said she wasn't involved in the auction, but they were quite interested in what happened."

"I know you don't believe in coincidences, and as a cop, I don't either. However, it may be a stretch to think they attacked Fiona and stole a box of buttons."

"Not if they believed there were valuable gemstones inside. I think after the box was stolen and the perpetrator was rushing through the alley, they dropped the cupcake liner, and perhaps the box lid flipped open, causing some of the contents to spill out.

They collected everything except for one lone item."

"Have you been back to the alley since you were caught snooping around?"

"No, but that's a great idea. We should head down there now while it's still sunny."

"Maybe you should leave that to the police?"

Beth stood. "Or not. You can join us if you wish to document it, should it become necessary."

Having found an exact number of pearls earlier, I doubted we would see any more. But it didn't hurt to look. "Are you coming with us?"

"On one condition: you can look, but if you see anything remotely resembling a clue, show it to me, and I'll mark the spot."

I looked at Beth, and she nodded. "Sounds fair."

I brought my cell phone to take pictures, and Beth said, "I'm going to have Dad come over once he closes the shop. I want to bring him up to speed."

Eddie held the door open as we walked out. "That's a good idea. Maybe he can keep an eye on you ladies while I'm at work."

"There's no mischief we can get into tonight since we've checked off everything on my clue list."

He chuckled. "Doubtful. The name Teddy is on the board; you didn't mention him."

"Supposedly, a dealer from New Hampshire stopped by Fiona's shop a week before she received the boxes from the auction house. He was specifically looking for buttons and was curious how quickly she'd unpack them when the boxes arrived. I don't think he was the person who broke the window. Based on Fiona's description, he's too tall and older. Our person was fit and lean."

He nodded. "There's a woman who can describe the first person who walked into her shop over thirty years ago. You can be sure she nailed it down to hair and eye color."

"That's a handy skill," Beth said.

"I'll message you the information I have. Could you use your sources to verify whether Teddy is involved in the second-hand shop business or if he is up to something suspicious?"

"I will add it to my to-do list tonight once I reach the station."

We entered the alley between Twice Loved and Whistlers Inn. Eddie pulled out his flashlight, although I wasn't sure why since the sun was at our backs and other than on the opposite side of the dumpster, there wasn't a shadow in sight.

"Show me exactly where you found the pearl."

"Follow me." I hurried down the narrow alley and pointed to the front wheel of the container. "Right here, but it was picked up today. Nothing else should be in the area."

He checked around the metal bin, sweeping the flashlight over the ground from one side to the other. Beth and I spread out, each heading to a different side of the alley. I remained on the left, aligned with the garbage container.

What is that? I knelt on the gravel. There was a small stick close by. I used that to push aside a paper, and I called to Eddie. "Take a look at this."

He and Beth came over. She said, "What did you find?"

"An old crochet-style shank button. This resembles something from an old box of buttons. My grandmother has all kinds of single buttons from back in the day. People used to save these to repurpose." I scuttled to another spot and pointed to the ground. "Look here, a flat mother of pearl button, and this one looks like it could be brass."

He knelt beside me. "I'll admit it, I was wrong. Don't touch anything while I call the station to get someone over here to document the scene."

The moment he walked away, I started taking pictures of the buttons next to the dumpster. I slipped my phone back into my pocket as he returned.

"This is great work. As much as I know you'd like to stay, could you please return to your apartment? In less than ten minutes, we'll have several officers scouring the area for additional clues."

I frowned. "We'll stay out of the way."

He shook his head. "Not this time. But I appreciate everything you've done to advance this case. This is a solid lead, especially considering the very expensive pearl." He patted his chest pocket.

"Will you tell us if you find anything else?"

He gave me a long look. "You know I can't share details about an open investigation."

With a shrug, I said, "Can't blame a girl for trying." I bobbed my head toward the street. "Come on Beth."

She walked beside me as we exited the

alley without glancing back. "What are you up to now?"

"I have Julia and Sienna's measurements."

"I don't understand how that helps us?"

"I'm a dress designer with computer software. I can input measurements to create outfits. Why can't I use the same software to build a profile and see if we can match that to a window person?"

Sucking in a sharp breath, she asked, "That's possible?"

"I've never done anything like this before, but I can't see why it wouldn't work. It might take longer than designing an outfit, but if I create the clothing to be dark and close to the body, combined with accurate measurements, we might just create something useful."

"Will you share it with Eddie?"

"If we get a match, absolutely. If it doesn't work, I don't want him to think I'm an over-the-top sofa sleuth."

"Dad should bring dinner. I think it's going to be an interesting evening."

"If he wants, I can order something and pay for it if he'll pick it up."

"Nah. He's going to offer to cook. Do you have groceries?"

"How about you look, let him know what I have, and he can decide from there. He only needs to come over if he wants to; there's no pressure from us."

"When I tell him what's happening, after I swear him to secrecy, of course, he'll be dying of curiosity to see this design software."

"As a side note, this software will also be useful when we work on pairing knitwear with my designs. As our first win–win for the collaboration between B and C, we can refine what we want to offer before either of us picks up a needle."

19

———————

I could hear pots clanging in the kitchen as Ethan prepared a seafood stir-fry. Beth sat at the edge of the sofa while I worked on the design program. "I think I've got something useful," I said, patting the spot next to me. "Have a look."

Herman hovered behind us. "I had no idea designing was this sophisticated. When I went to school, it was all hand drawings and making toiles."

Beth said, "Explain to me what I'm looking at."

"What I did was input Julia's measurements into the program and create a quick design of basic slim-fitting pants and a top in a dark color. This resembles what the window person was wearing." I pulled up my phone with the footage and held it to the laptop screen. When I compared the images, disappointment settled over me. "We can see that the figure I created is more curvaceous."

"Could you adjust the measurements so we can see how the other body shape would look?"

"It'll take a couple of minutes."

"This is impressive; it definitely saves time. Do you use this to create practice garments or to present ideas to a client?"

Herman grumbled from behind us, saying, "I have the same question."

I smiled. "I guess some designers might, but I love taking fabric and creating the toile; it's the sample. This way, I can fit the fabric on a less expensive option, especially if the customer is unhappy with the design after they try it on. It saves time and money."

"I'm glad to hear you do things the traditional way," Herman said as he drifted toward the kitchen. "I'll be back. I want to see what Ethan's whipping up for dinner. I miss his cooking."

After updating the information and recalculating the new body shape, I compared it to the camera footage. "The height looks good, but Sienna is more slender than this person. Darn. I hoped we could show this to Eddie and point to one of the ladies. Not that I wanted the bride to feel guilty but given how they reacted to the conversation about the theft of items from the Madison family, if I were Sienna, I'd be more curious about the reason for it."

"Clues never line up in a linear fashion." Ethan entered with a plate of cheese, crackers, and grapes. "It would be nice, but they don't." He set the plate on the table in front of us. "Dinner won't be ready for forty-five minutes. I just started the rice. To keep your brainpower up, here's a small snack." He sat across from us. "What are you working on that didn't give you the desired results?"

I guided Ethan through my clues and why I had created simulated people. "I wanted the person with the window to resemble one of the ladies, and I didn't think it would be un-reasonable for the other to be her ac-complice."

"Excellent deduction. That's something I would have explored, too. Naturally, it wouldn't have been aided by a design pro-gram; I would have used an illustrator instead."

I nibbled on a piece of cheese. "Are we missing something?"

He scanned the board. "Teddy from New Hampshire. What's that story?"

"Initially, I thought it could be tied back to this current issue. The man was looking for vintage buttons and was especially interested to have the first look at the Madison acquisition. However, I can't find any record of his store online. The only real connection is that they're all from New Hampshire, but that's a large state with a lot of secondhand and antique stores and even more people."

He smiled. "True, and Teddy could have changed his store name at any time. Did you try calling the number again?"

"No, should I? Eddie has the information. I thought he would follow up."

"Leave it to him. Tell me what you've discovered that you haven't shared with him." He grinned. "Beth has a bit of her father in her, and you, well, you've got a knack for looking at information with a twist."

I looked at Beth, and she laughed. "I didn't tell him what we found, only that we were going to withhold a juicy detail from Eddie until tomorrow."

"If we tell you, can you keep a secret? It's not like I'm, we're, not going to tell him, but we need a few more details before we do."

"This isn't about a button box, is it?"

"Not exactly. The pearl I gave Eddie tonight was from the stolen box. At least, I'm betting it was since we found other buttons near where the dumpster was. Picture this: the perp was zipping through the alley and tossed some trash on the ground. The box was jostled, spilling some of the contents. He or she may have tried to pick them all up, but they didn't want to draw attention to themselves since it was still daylight. Blending in with people strolling on the street or beach was more important. In their haste, they left behind one single, rare sea pearl, which I discovered when I took the trash out."

He coughed to cover his laughter. "I heard about your very late-night trash dump."

"What can I say? When you have chores to do, you get them done." With a shrug of my shoulders, I got up, took another wedge of cheese, and moved to the board. "After confirming that it was worth a lot of money, Beth and I discussed it and decided to check in with Fiona. At that moment, I asked if I could look through the remaining three boxes that hadn't been unpacked yet."

I picked up a marker next to box one and jotted down a question mark. "We have no idea if there was anything else of value beyond the hypothesis that it contained a pearl, which wasn't a button. For box two, there was nothing but fabric." I wrote *ZIP*. "Moving on to box three, I must say this box was a rip-off. Most of the hats and gloves were moth-eaten and were only good for the trash bin. I suppose that can happen when purchasing a box of items from an auction." I wrote *YUCK* on that line. "Now we can discuss the final box. At this point, neither Beth nor I held much hope since we'd been operating under the premise that we were searching for something special that could have been used as a button. This is also in light of the tidbit that Sienna mentioned about how her grandmother became very upset with her and Tristan when they played dress-up with the wedding gown and took it away from them so they couldn't play with it any longer. They didn't see it again until recently when the buttons were missing.

"This is quite a tale of supposition."

I grinned. "I'm not done with the grand finale." I added, *Ding, Ding, Ding,* on the fourth line. "This was a box of costume jewelry. I'm not sure if you've ever watched an unboxing video when a secondhand or even a vintage jeweler opens a mystery bag or tote they purchased from an auction." He shook his head. "Typically, they dump out the contents and sort through what is broken, real silver or gold, or excellent vintage pieces, but the real hope is there's a true gem, no pun intended, in the box."

Lifting his brows, Ethan leaned forward, his arms resting on his thighs. "So, our thief, in an attempt to find the valuable pieces, stole the wrong box?"

I nodded. "That's what I think. In the typical costume pieces, we found nineteen gems, which I believe are part of a set matching the first one I discovered under the dumpster."

"Well, that is a solid working theory. And the stones you found are pearls that you want to have appraised before turning them over to Eddie?"

"Yes. At least Fiona is safe. Since I have the pearls, there's no need for anyone to bother her again."

"Claudia, whoever it was doesn't know that you have them. As far as they know, Fiona hasn't unpacked that box yet. There might be a return visit in her future."

That was a wrinkle I hadn't considered. "And I put the boxes back in her storage room."

Beth stood. "Dad, please keep an eye on things. We'll head over to Fiona's and put on a big show to remove the shipping boxes."

"If anyone is watching her place, they'll know I've taken the costume jewelry back here."

"You'll put a target on your back to protect Fiona?"

My gut clenched, but without hesitation, I nodded. "Ethan, it's the best way to protect her."

"No. The best way is to turn it over as evidence to the police and tell Eddie what you've done."

I shook my head. "I can't tell him about the new stones, but I will give him the boxes. I'll text him and ask him to meet us at Fiona's."

"He may already be on his way there since you mentioned what you discovered, and they are processing the alley."

My cell pinged, and I scanned the screen. "It's Eddie. He's asking me to meet him at Twice Loved."

"Good thing we were just about to leave." Beth patted Ethan's shoulder. "We'll be back soon."

I handed Ethan the remote for the television. "For company."

"Hey," Herman floated in, "I'll keep him company."

I winked at my ghostly companion as I walked past him. "I'll feed Lola when I get back, so don't let her convince you that she's going to die of starvation."

He snorted and whistled for the little minx. She trotted into the room, jumped onto his lap, and started to purr.

"Someone's happy you're hanging out." Beth laughed and said to me after I closed the door, "Lola adores my dad."

"She's a great judge of character." We descended the steps. Eddie was waiting for us at the bottom.

"Thanks for agreeing to go with me."

"I was about to call you anyway. Ethan suggested that we create a big deal about getting those last boxes out of Fiona's place. If anyone is considering a return trip, they'll know she doesn't have anything from that shipment."

He fell in step next to us. "You believe this is related to that shipment?"

I saw the set to his jawline. He was all business. Police business. "Yes, I do. Don't you? Too many little things are adding up. However, I don't think Julia or Sienna are the vandals."

"Why?"

"I can show you later. I created mockups using their measurements in a design program I work with and compared these designs to the footage. They don't match."

He gave a quick nod. "I'd like to look into that later."

We approached Twice Loved from the rear. Fiona stood in the open doorway, waving as she waited for us.

"I was surprised to get your call, Eddie."

"I apologize for bothering you, Fiona. We are following up on the incident that occurred on Sunday and would like to review the contents of the remaining three boxes you purchased at the auction."

"Certainly. I have them just inside the storeroom."

She spoke in a loud, clear voice. Was this to ensure that if anyone were lurking, they would overhear the conversation?

"Come inside."

We entered the shop, and she left the door open. Again, speaking loudly, she said, "I threw out a few hats I won't be able to sell due to moth holes." She passed the fabric and hat box to Eddie, and I picked up the last box.

"Eddie, would it be all right if I looked through the box with necklaces and bracelets? I'm hoping to find a brooch for an outfit I'm putting together."

He narrowed his eyes. "Can't it wait until after we catalog the items?"

"I know it bends protocol, and if there's something suitable, I won't take it. I'm just curious, that's all." My eyes widened as I tilted my head, hoping he'd realize I was trying to draw more attention to myself and not to Fiona.

She said, "I haven't had a chance to look in there. I'm sure it wouldn't hurt anything if Claudia peeked."

He hung his head. I could see his shoulders shake with laughter. Softly, he said, "I'm only interrupting the chain of evidence, which, if I were to make an educated guess, has already been tampered with."

I remained mum. Beth snickered, and Fiona said, "Officer Eddie, you have what you need."

He opened the box and handed me the case inside. "Stay here where I can supervise, and if you want to take a picture of the brooch, you can."

"Thank you." Knowing there was nothing of value left in the box, I decided to play it up. "The light in here isn't very bright. Would it be okay if I went outside?"

He threw up his hands. "Why not? So far, nothing about this case has gone per regulation." He picked up the three boxes, and I carried the case to the small table next to the stairs leading to Fiona's apartment.

I pulled out a chair and sat down. Beth and Fiona joined me. Eddie glanced around and nodded. I had the feeling someone was watching us but I didn't know from where, exactly.

Beth had her cell out. "I'll take pictures for you."

"Great, I appreciate the help."

I took out several cuff bracelets that I had seen earlier and set them aside, along with the chunky necklaces and earrings. Then I said, "There are some loose stones at the bottom of the case." At this point, only Fiona and Beth knew what had been there a few hours earlier. Eddie didn't pay any attention to what I was saying as he continued to scan the area.

"Did you find the brooch you were looking for?" he asked.

"Nope." I glanced up and saw he was looking toward the bay. I pretended to scoop some items from the box and slip them into my pants pocket. I did it once more, satisfied that my performance was worthy of an Oscar, I closed the lid.

"Eddie, thank you for indulging me. Sadly, there wasn't anything in there that I could use for the design." I pushed back the chair and handed him the box.

He handed Fiona a slip of paper. "As soon as we've completed our investigation, I'll return the items to you."

"I hope you find the culprit, but I feel safer knowing that you have the boxes."

I nodded to Beth and cleared my throat. "We should get back to my place. I need to tie up a few loose ends before dinner." I patted my pocket, ensuring that all inquisitive eyes zeroed in on me, supposedly making off with the pearls.

20

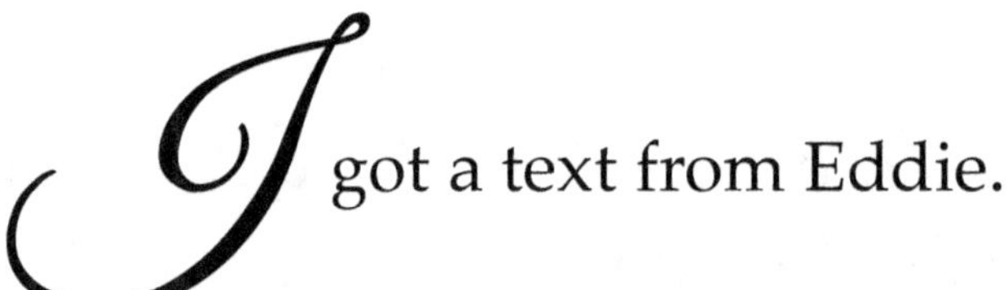 got a text from Eddie.

I'm not sure what you were doing at Fiona's, but please don't take any unnecessary chances.

I appreciated his concern; however, I wanted to make it clear to whoever was hiding in the shadows that Fiona didn't have the pearls. If anyone wanted to come after someone tonight, it should be me.

I sent back, *Protecting Fiona.*

Once we were inside my apartment, Beth said, "You put a target on your back."

"It'll be fine. I have cameras, and with you and Ethan around, it's not like anyone will come knocking on my door demanding that I hand over the gems."

"Then I'm staying the night." She sat down in a kitchen chair.

Ethan looked between us. "Why so grim?"

"Claudia is jeopardizing her safety for some stupid pearls."

"Maybe this is something that should be discussed." He pointed for me to have a seat. "We have time before dinner's ready."

"It's no big deal." With a shrug, I sat in the chair he pulled out. "While we were at Fiona's and Eddie made a big show of taking the boxes she bought from the auction, I pretended to pocket some items from the last box."

"I see."

"Ethan, what would you have done? We were being watched. Not that I can prove it, but you know that hinky feeling?"

He nodded.

"Well, we felt it the whole time we were at her place."

Beth said, "She's right. There was someone, but I didn't see where they were hiding. Eddie did, too."

"I pretended to pocket the pearls since, for all anyone knew, Fiona had already unpacked that box and stashed the valuables."

"There was no way for Eddie to comment on them since they weren't there, and he knows nothing about them." He shook his head. "Claudia, you need to tell him what you know and, more importantly, turn over the pearls to him. You're withholding crucial evidence. If for no other reason, do it to protect Fiona and yourself."

Beth's rosy cheeks went pale. "It's potentially two hundred thousand reasons."

"What?" Ethan handed me his cell. "Call Eddie."

"Can I call him after dinner? I want to talk to Gavin first and get his opinion. This way, I'll have more to share with Eddie."

"Who's Gavin?"

"Dad, he's the antique jeweler in Portland who told us what the first pearl was worth. If the others are of similar quality, it's reasonable to assume they're part of a set."

"I'm not thrilled with the stall. But I guess a short delay will be okay since he's logging evidence he collected."

"And you're both here. I'm safe."

Ethan didn't speak for what felt like an eternity.

"Dinner will be ready in ten minutes. Will that give you enough time to speak with the man from Portland?"

I nodded. "Yes." I got up. "I'm going downstairs to call him."

"Do you want company?" Beth asked.

"Sure." I opened the door to the shop.

Herman was hovering inside the stairwell. "Ethan's right. Give the pearls to Eddie."

She was behind me. "There's one thing that I can't figure out."

"Can I guess what you're thinking? I might be mulling over the same question."

She laughed. "The pearls you found are too large to be buttons."

"Exactly. One half inch is just over 12 mm, and a seed pearl is typically 2 mm, which is less than one-eighth of an inch. They are vastly different and are used in various types of garments. Fastening would be very awkward unless it were a flat button, especially on a wedding gown. Therefore, I want to measure the opening of the loops on the dress and examine the spacing between them. I might be able to calculate what was used on the original dress."

I flipped on the overhead workroom lights. The antique gown was resting on a dress form, and I was relieved that I hadn't begun the cleaning process yet. It was dry.

"What can I do to help?"

"While I measure, could you take some pictures with my phone? I'll hold up buttons of various sizes. I believe this could be important for Eddie's investigation."

"Do you think someone from the Madison family will come forward to claim them?"

"Anything is possible but highly unlikely. They'll wait until the boxes are returned to Fiona and then ask about buying the box of costume jewelry, waxing poetic about its sentimental value. They'll hope she hasn't discovered the truth."

As I developed my theory, I gathered a small metal ruler I often used, arranged the button sizes from the smallest to largest, and positioned a bright spotlight at the back of the gown.

I held up the ruler and took my first measurement. "It looks like the loops are three-quarters and one inch apart." I jotted that down. I picked several buttons and placed them against the back of the dress. "Could you help me lay the dress on the worktable? It's difficult to visualize button spacing."

We removed the dress from the form and laid it flat. I repositioned the light and placed various-sized buttons in groups of three, starting with 3 mm and going up to 9.5 mm.

Beth leaned closer. "What can you see by this?"

"The smaller the button, the farther apart they'd have to be, which would have kept the back closed. If there had been a zipper, you could get away with fewer buttons." I tapped the mid-back of the gown. "See here the 6-mm button and the loops? It's almost perfectly aligned." I looked up at her. This means that the pearl couldn't have been a button; more likely, it was a necklace."

"So, they weren't attached to the dress?"

"I'm not sure, but I don't think they could have been, but Julia said her grandmother cut them off. They must have been secured to the gown otherwise that statement makes no sense."

"Dinner!" Ethan called down to us.

I nodded toward the stairs. "Go on up. I'll call Gavin first."

"Don't take too long." Beth closed the door to give me some privacy, and Herman drifted in.

"Hello there." I smiled at my ghostly uncle.

"Claudia, would you like to review what you've discovered before calling your new friend?"

I perched on the edge of a stool. "I'm confused about why someone would say that pearls were used as buttons on this gown. They're too large."

"This dress is very old. Based on the design, I would estimate it dates back to the turn of the twentieth century. You're correct about the button size and spacing. But consider the pearls. If they're worth so much today, they would have been valuable a hundred years ago, too. Again, considering money: if you discovered pearls worth fifteen thousand dollars, and as a baseline from more than a century ago, why would they need to be attached to a dress?"

My eyes widened. "They were stolen?"

He nodded. "Possibly."

I pressed my hand to my forehead. "Can an old crime still be on the record?"

"During World War II, artwork was stolen, and when discovered in various personal collections, it was returned to its rightful owners."

"Oh-Em-Gee." I paced around the table. "I must speak to Gavin." I pulled the card from my pocket and dialed. It was after the shop would have closed. Maybe this was his cell number.

"Hello?"

"Gavin? This is Claudia Grant. I visited your shop earlier today with the sea pearl."

He chuckled. "I remember; it's not every

day that a beautiful woman enters my shop with a rare gem."

The compliment was nice, but this wasn't a social call. "I apologize for the interruption, but if I found nineteen more pearls that resemble the one I showed you today, from the same auction lot, would it be unreasonable to think they're worth a similar value?"

"Do they have the same look and feel as the first?"

"Yes." The word fell softly from my lips.

"I can't say for certain until I examine them, but it would be a safe assumption that they are. Will you bring the others in for me to appraise?"

"I hope to stop in tomorrow." That was, if Eddie didn't take them.

"I look forward to it, not just to the pearls but also to see you again."

Was he flirting with me? I cleared my throat. "Thank you; until tomorrow."

I switched off the overhead light and glanced out the front window. Julia stood with her hand raised as if she were going to knock on my door, but then she suddenly crumpled to the ground.

I dashed through the salon and flung the door open. Her face was pale, and she remained unresponsive when I called her name. "Julia," I tapped her cheek gently, "Open your eyes." The door closed with a soft *thud*.

Rubbing her hands between mine, I said, "Come on, Julia. Look at me."

Her eyes fluttered open. "Claudia? I'm not sure what happened." She struggled to sit up, and I wrapped my arm around her back for support. "I felt dizzy."

"You're going to be fine. We should get inside, and I'll get you a glass of water." I looked around the street. "Are you alone?"

"No." Tristan emerged from behind the large planter by the door. He extended his hand to help Julia up. "We needed to talk with you before you made a decision you might regret."

"I'm— I'm not following you."

He gestured to my pockets. "Empty them." He held out a linen bag.

"I don't understand." I turned out my pockets, showing him the lint-covered seams.

"Where are they? Did you stash them in the workroom? We know you've been down here for a while now."

"Have you been watching me?"

He snorted. "Since Sunday. And tonight, when you rifled through a box that didn't belong to you. As a woman living alone, you should be more aware of your surroundings. You never know who might be out there."

Stammering, I said, "I haven't done anything wrong."

"Ah, but you did. Taking something that doesn't belong to you without paying for it is stealing."

"You should know. Breaking into a store after hours, taking a box, and hitting a woman on the head is a crime." I took the opportunity to scan the street. At dinnertime midweek, downtown, as usual, resembled a ghost town.

"He never meant to hurt the old woman. She wasn't supposed to be in the shop after it closed."

It clicked. Had I been paying attention when Sienna and Julia were at the dress fitting, I would have heard the *old* reference to Fiona and the attack. I hadn't mentioned either bit of information.

"But he did. I must ask, why? The supposed buttons that Julia mentioned when she first came in with the gown don't add up, and neither does the condition of the dress."

Tristan growled, "I don't have the energy to explain this to you. Just give me what belongs to my family, and we'll drive off into the sunset."

"Brother, being rude won't get us what is rightfully ours." Sienna walked up the sidewalk from the inn. "I must apologize for my twin; his patience could use some improvement."

"The three of you are in this together?"

Sienna nodded. "Teamwork does make the dream happen."

Julia looked between her fiancé and future sister-in-law. "The pearls aren't in her pocket."

Sienna grabbed my upper arm and squeezed. "Where did you put them?"

"I don't have them."

She sneered. "We had a perfect view of your little get-together outside the second-hand shop. I saw your hand reach for items in one of the boxes and stuff your pocket. So, if they're empty, the gems must be inside. Shall we?"

I wished I hadn't closed the door to the apartment. From experience, I knew that sound didn't travel well in this building. Herman had soundproofed the apartment against street noise. My secret weapon was my ghost—not that he could communicate with Ethan and Beth.

"Stop stalling and open the door." Sienna jerked my arm.

Julia whimpered. "No one's supposed to get hurt."

"No one will if Claudia gives us back our property." Tristan pulled the door open, and we entered. "Keep your voices down. We don't want that father–daughter duo coming downstairs." He withdrew a small handgun.

My heart stopped beating. Herman zipped around the room. "This is not good, Claudia. Call out to Ethan."

"People, I don't have the pearls—neither in my pocket nor in my shop. I looked through the box but didn't take anything. The police have them."

"You're lying," Tristan advanced threateningly.

Julia said, "Maybe we saw what we hoped to see. It's not that big of a deal. We should walk away."

"Never," Sienna grumbled, her eyes narrowed and nodded at the gown on the table.

"Do you know what's so special about that gown?"

"It belonged to your family?"

"It was used to smuggle an entire strand of sea pearls from beneath my great-great-grandfather's nose. He forbade my great-grandmother to marry the man she loved. Before stripping her of her jewelry, she dismantled a necklace that had belonged to her mother and had it sewn as decorative buttons onto that gown. When she eloped, she took the dress along with a small fortune to start her new life. They used the pearls, one at a time, to live the life they dreamed of."

"Then how did they end up coming off the dress?"

"Our Nana believed she was safeguarding what remained of our legacy. When she saw us wearing the gown, she cut the buttons off and stored them and the dress in her armoire. Nobody knew what had happened to it until after she had her live-in companion box up most of her belongings for auction. The companion thought she was doing the right thing to help us after Nana passed."

"And no one realized that one of the cartons contained rare pearls?"

Herman had vanished into the ceiling, and I searched the room for any weapon to defend myself. Unfortunately, all I found nearby were bolts of fabric—and a pair of scissors was no match for the gun casually aimed at me.

Tristan said, "Finally, you figured it out."

"Then, why didn't you go to Fiona and ask her if you could purchase the items instead of stealing them? She's a reasonable person."

"Once she examined the contents, curiosity about the pearls arose. They were too beautiful to believe they were imitations. It was only a matter of time before she had them appraised. Moreover, buying in good faith from an auction is part of the agreement. What you buy, you own, even if the item's value is significantly higher." Sienna gestured to the workroom. "Let's take a quick look, shall we?"

I remained still and calculated how quickly I could grab a bolt of fabric to disarm Tristan. "Who clobbered Fiona?" Julia had said it was Tristian but I wanted him to confess.

"Can you forget about that?"

I took a step back. "No, not if you're asking for my help. I need answers, too. Like who broke the window and set off fireworks?"

He groaned. "You're annoying," he said and glared at Sienna. "You tell her."

In that split second, I twirled, grabbed the bolt of muslin, and swung as hard as I could, connecting the fabric with his wrist, hip, and midsection. The gun went off. I pushed Julia into Sienna, pulled open the front door, and screamed. "FIRE!"

Julia and Sienna shoved Tristan aside and rushed to the street as I continued to scream "FIRE, repeatedly."

He limped after them just as Ethan and Beth emerged from the alley.

Ethan had his gun drawn. "Freeze."

The sound of sirens was music to my ears.

"Claudia, come over here." Ethan waved the gun at the trio. "You three stay close and don't make any sudden movements."

Julia broke out in tears. "We didn't mean any harm."

Tristan cradled his hand against his body. "That woman broke my wrist."

A police cruiser screeched to a halt. Eddie jumped out and strode over. "Ethan, what's going on?"

"Claudia, did you crack the case?" His question and glance in my direction made me grin.

"Eddie, they broke into Fiona's, stole the box, assaulted her, and have been staying at the inn waiting for another chance."

Narrowing her eyes, Sienna said, "That's your word against three."

I gave her a victorious smile. "That's not

quite true. You see, I have security cameras inside my shop that are voice-activated. All the police need to do is review and save the footage as proof of your guilt."

Tristan glared at Sienna. "What a brilliant idea, sis. Push her back into her shop."

Rhonda Perkins arrived in another police cruiser and stepped out. She glanced between me and Eddie, who was reading Miranda rights to Julia, Sienna, and Tristan.

"What happened?"

"Claudia obtained a taped confession on her security camera concerning the incident at Twice Loved." He winked at me. I was grateful that Rhonda hadn't seen that.

I kept my distance from the three but said, "There's just one thing that needs to be cleared up."

Eddie said, "What's that?"

"Tristan, did you break the window on Fiona's doorstep?"

Stone-faced, he said, "Maybe."

"Julia, did you set off the fireworks?"

With a shake of her head, she muttered. "It was Sienna."

She lunged at Julia, and Rhonda grabbed her by the arm, escorting her to the back of the cruiser before returning for Julia. Eddie placed Tristan in the back of his car before coming over to me. He touched my arm. "Are you okay?"

I nodded and took a deep, ragged breath. "Is there any chance you could find Tristan's gun in the salon? It went off when I hit him with a bolt of fabric, and he dropped it."

"You got it."

Beth and Ethan wrapped their arms around me. He said, "Dinner's getting cold."

I laughed. "It's a good thing I have a microwave."

Saturday arrived, and the weather was perfect for a fall festival. Beth suggested dressing in layers while looking cute, so I applied a swish of mauve lipstick and blotted my lips.

Herman hovered in the hallway. "Great outfit! I love pairing a sweater from Beth's shop with the dark washed jeans."

"Thank you; it's one of the ideas we're developing for next year's fall line."

"I approve." He drifted down the hall, and I followed him.

"Herman, thank you for alerting Ethan the other night. Without him, I wouldn't have been able to keep the suspects gathered in one place."

"It took some effort to get the front window ajar, but my timing was impeccable. You yelled 'fire' the first time at the right moment. I wondered why you didn't yell 'police' or 'help.'"

"Grandma always said, 'If you need help, yelling fire is the best thing to do. Since a blaze out of control affects many people, it will prompt them to call 9-1-1.'"

He nodded. "She's a brilliant woman."

A knock on my door sent butterflies dancing in my stomach. This was more nerve racking than standing my ground against the gun-wielding Tristan. "That's Eddie."

"Have a good time today. You deserve to have some fun."

Through the glass, I saw Eddie standing on the deck. I opened the door. "Hello."

He spun around and handed me a vase of black-eyed Susans. "These are for you." He kissed my cheek. "Thank you for being my sort-of date today."

Heat flushed my cheeks. "I'm happy you asked me." I placed the flowers on the table inside the apartment and closed the door. "I've never been to a fall festival."

"Well, it's a good thing I have. The even better news is that your chances of getting involved in another police case are almost nil. Pembroke Cove has an excellent reputation for being a safe and dull town—except for the good fun."

I laughed. "I think Beth and I are retiring

as sofa sleuths, and we'll leave that to the professionals."

"That sounds like a great idea." His blue-gray eyes sparkled, and he extended his hand. "Ready?"

I took it and smiled. "For anything."

If you loved Buttons & Burglary, help other readers find this book:
Please leave a review now!
Are you ready to read more from the Lily and the gang in Pembroke?
Keep reading for a sneak peek at
Pleats & Poison
A Craft and Ghost Cozy Mystery
A Dress Designer Cozy Mystery Series
Order Now
Or
Shop at Lucinda Race

Lucinda

I hope you want to keep up with my crazy antics of writing, gardening, cooking, and life with the pups.

Not ready to stop reading yet? If you sign up for my newsletter at www.lucindarace.com/ newsletter, you will receive an excerpt for Cookies & Capers, the introduction of when Lily met Milo right away, as my thank-you gift for choosing to get my newsletter.

Pleats & Poison

Enjoy this humorous, small-town, psychic, cozy mystery by best-selling and award-winning Lucinda Race.

She didn't want to talk to ghosts or investigate a murder.

Claudia Grant didn't want to talk to another

ghost or two—and she definitely didn't want to investigate a murder.

Hosting Thanksgiving dinner for seven guests—and one ghost—is all in a day's work for Claudia Grant. Between whipping up her famous mac and cheese and debuting her boutique's latest fall fashion, Claudia's ready to impress her visiting mom and stylish grandmother. Her cozy coastal town of Drakes Bay is the perfect backdrop for family, food, and fresh starts—especially when Gram falls in love with a pleated skirt and sweater ensemble from Claudia's shop.

But when a spilled glass of orange juice leads to a shocking discovery—a guest at the neighboring Whistlers Inn is found dead, and the very same pleated skirt wrapped around her neck—Claudia's holiday cheer unravels fast.

Now, with her best friend Beth and a ghostly sidekick in tow, Claudia must piece together a tangled mystery before the killer skips town... and before the secrets hidden in the folds come back to haunt them all.

She'd rather be sewing hemlines than following clues—but if Claudia can't stitch together the truth in time, someone else might be the next to check out… permanently.

Pleats & Poison
A Craft and Ghost Cozy Mystery
Order Now

A FREE STORY FOR YOU

Have you enjoyed Buttons & Burglary? Not ready to stop reading yet? If you sign up for my newsletter at www.lucindarace.com/newsletter, you will receive Cookies & Capers, which is the start of Lily and Milo's adventure in the Bookstore Cozy Mystery Series, as my thank-you gift for choosing to receive my newsletter.

Cookies & Capers

I stood in front of the old wood and glass door as I pocketed the keys to the Cozy Nook Bookshop. Aunt Mimi had signed her bookstore over to me. She said it felt like giving me her baby. But I loved the shop as much as my aunt did. We had worked together for the last twelve years. After attending the University of Maine, I had a degree in history and education. I had always wanted to be a teacher, but jobs were scarce and after substituting for a few years, I moved back to my hometown of Pembroke, Maine, and Aunt Mimi hired me as soon as I unpacked my suitcase.

Spending time with my aunt, learning the business, had been the best experience. I offered to buy the shop when she wanted to retire, but she wouldn't hear of it. As long as she had free books for life, and her long-term boyfriend Nate, she said it was a fair deal. From my point of view, I had built-in backup for years to come.

Now that I was the bookshop owner, Aunt Mimi was no longer coming in every day which meant her cat, Phoenix, wasn't either and the space felt empty without a kitty lying in the window or skulking about as kitties do. I was off to the Pembroke Animal Palace to see if I could find a match.

It was a short walk in the bright noonday sun. The spring air from the ocean carried a tang of salt, but the breeze was refreshing. I waved to one of my best friends, Gage Erikson, as he drove past in his police-issued sedan. My heart fluttered in my chest.

He was a detective on the force. Not that we had much crime in our small seaside town. But one of these days I was going to get brave and tell him I had been carrying a torch for him since we were in ninth grade. What's the worst thing that could happen? We'd still be best friends, right?

I continued down the brick sidewalk, waving to William North from the Sweet Spot

Bakery. He was sweeping the area around the small bistro tables in front of the bakery. William was wearing a large pristine white apron and a wide smile. A deep inhale confirmed my suspicion. He was baking cookies. My mouth watered. I did a half turn and went back to where he was finishing up. "Good morning, William." I bobbed my head in the shop's direction. "What is that tantalizing smell?"

He held open the brightly polished glass door. "One of your favorites, Lily. Chocolate chip and pecan cookies. Can I interest you in one before you continue on your mission?"

I gave him a side-look. "Mission?"

He chuckled. "Over the years my Lulu had said you had two speeds, strolling and purposeful. Just now it was purposeful so hence you're on a mission."

"I'm going to the shelter, hoping to find a kitty. The shop is lonely now that Phoenix is home every day with Aunt Mimi, and I think a cat napping in the window adds an air of serenity to the place."

"Unless you're allergic."

He had a point, but I was not willing to be deterred. I smiled. "I'm always happy to deliver to a customer." I leaned over the glass bakery case, like a kid pressing her nose against the candy case. "You made sugar cookies too and frosted them?" I sighed. I was going to need to exercise more if he continued to bake all my favorites. He was smiling at me as I looked up. "Are the chocolate pecan ready?"

He wiggled his eyebrows. "I have a tray cooling in the back."

"Then can I have one of those and a sugar cookie, but to go?"

With a flick of his wrist, he snapped open a white bakery bag and called over his shoulder. "Jerilyn, would you please bring out the last batch of cookies?"

I heard a muffled, coming, and smiled.

"It's good that Jerilyn stayed on." I said nothing about his beloved wife Lulu. Rumor had it she was ill and not doing well.

He nodded. "It is. She's a hard worker and excellent with the customers."

Jerilyn bustled in from the back room carrying a large stainless-steel tray. It was lined with parchment paper and cookies the size of the palm of my hand. It was going to taste so good with a hot cup of tea later.

William put two in the bag, along with two sugar cookies, and then he handed it to me. I paid for my cookies and thanked him. "Stop by the shop later. You might just get to meet my new fur baby."

"Sounds like a plan." He grinned and crossed his arms over his rounded midsection. "You're more like your aunt than you realize. Ever since she opened that bookshop, she's had a cat, too."

I paused, tucked the bakery bag in my tote, and with my hand on the door, I turned and gave him a wide grin. "And now it's time I carry on the tradition." With a jaunty wave, I called, "Wish me luck."

Cookies & Capers is only available by signing up for my newsletter – sign up for it here at www.lucindarace.com/newsletter

LOVE TO READ?

**All ebooks and paperback copies can be ordered from my website at:
Shop at Lucinda Race**

Cozy Mystery Books
A Bookstore Cozy Mystery Series
Books & Bribes
It was an ordinary day until the book of Practical Magic conked Lily on the head causing her to see stars. And then she discovered her cat, Milo, could talk.

Catnaps & Crimes

The fun continues as Lily practices her magic and needs to investigate another murder.

Tea & Trouble

A fall festival, reading tea leaves and a few clues propel Lily into a new murder investigation.

Scares & Dares

What goes wrong at a haunted house is anything but expected until Lily starts following the clues.

Holidays & Homicide

Can Lily solve a murder before it ruins the holidays?

Leprechauns & Larceny

Will a dead leprechaun take the shine off the wedding?

Magicians & Murder

When four magicians roll into town for a show more than fun is on one person's mind.

Artifacts & Amulets
Milo has been keeping secrets, which can be deadly.

Cranberries & Criminals
Whose half-baked idea was it for bookstore owner and witch Lily Michaels to enter an amateur baking contest in her small town of Pembroke Cove, Maine?

Broomsticks & Blooms
The time has come for Lily to learn to fly.

Fishing & Forgery April 2025
A simple Sunday fishing adventure with friends where Lily and her friends reel in the big one.

Wands & Weddings May 2025
Lily and Gage are ready to tie the knot. But what's up with the coven's council? Can Lily unravel this new mystery before she says, I do.

Ghostly Gowns Series
A Paranormal Ghost Cozy Mystery Series
Ghost and Gowns June 2025
Buttons & Burglary July 2025
Ribbons & Robbery August 2025

Witches of Robins Pointe
A Paranormal Cozy Mystery Series
Inherited Magic & Murder January 2026
Touch of Magic February 2026
Waiting for Magic March 2026

Cowboys of River Junction
Second Chances in Montana
Twenty years later, Renee and Hank are back where they fell in love, but reality is like a spring frost, and is a long-distance relationship their only option for their second chance?

Stars Over Montana
The cowboy broke her heart, but he never stopped loving her. Now, she's back ready to run her grandfather's ranch...

Hiding in Montana
Can love flourish while danger lurks in the shadows?

Moonlight Over Montana
From the smoldering ash, she realizes he's all the family she and her daughter need.
rm can lead to love.

Price Family Romance Series
Breathe
Her dream come true may be the end of his...
Crush
The first time they met was fleeting; the second time restarted her heart.
<u>Blush</u>
He's always loved her but he left and now he's back...the question, does she still love him?
Vintage
He's an unexpected distraction, she gets his engine running...
<u>Bouquet</u>

Where do you go to heal your heart? You make the journey home...
The Last First Kiss
When life handed Kate lemons, she baked.
Ready to Soar
Kate will fight for love, won't she?
Love in the Looking Glass
Will Ellie's first love be her last or will she become a ghost like her father?
Magic in the Rain
Dani's plan of hiding in plain sight may not have been the best idea.
After All These Years
Arielle Clark is a famous artist with a painful past. When her first love comes to town, ghosts from the past are resurrected. But can the embers of love still linger after all these years?

Standalone Titles
Shamrocks are a Girl's Best Friend
Will a bit of Irish luck and a matchmaking uncle give Kelly and Tric a chance to find love?

The Matchmaker and The Marine
She vowed never to love again. His career in the Marines crushed his ability to love. Can undeniable chemistry and a leap of faith overcome their past?

<u>Sundaes on Sunday</u>
A widowed school teacher and the airline pilot whose little girl is determined to bring her daddy and the lady from the ice cream shop together for a second chance at love.

Barrett
Has the last man standing finally met his match?
Marie
Career-focused city girl discovers small town chances

Holiday Heart Wishes
Heartfelt wishes and holiday kisses…

<u>Holiday Heart Wishes</u>
Hockey, holidays, and a slap shot to the heart.

<u>Christmas in July</u>
She's the hometown girl with the hometown advantage. Right?

<u>A Secret Santa Christmas</u>
Christmas just isn't Holly's thing, but will a family secret help her find the true meaning of Christmas?

The Sugar Plum Inn
The chef and the restaurant critic are about to come face to face.

Holiday Romance Box Set
Sweet with a touch of heat holiday romance novels.

SOCIAL MEDIA

Follow Me on Social Media

Like my Facebook page
Join Lucinda's Heart Racer's Reader Group
on Facebook
Twitter @lucindarace
Instagram @lucindaraceauthor
BookBub
Goodreads
Pinterest
YouTube

ABOUT THE AUTHOR

Award-winning and best-selling author Lucinda Race is a lifelong fan of fiction who fell in love with cozy mysteries and romance novels as a young girl. While her childhood friends dreamed of becoming doctors and engineers, Lucinda was already dreaming of crafting captivating novels filled with heart, hope, and happily ever afters.

Though her writing journey began with nonfiction, her passion for storytelling never wavered. She returned to her true calling—

creating the beloved McKenna Family Romance series and the Paranormal Cozy Nook Bookstore Series—writing the kinds of stories she loves to read. Whether she's weaving a heartwarming romance or a paranormal cozy mystery, her fingers practically fly across the keyboard.

Lucinda lives in the rolling hills of western Massachusetts with her two little dogs—a miniature long-haired dachshund and a shih tzu mix rescue—who are always by her side. When she's not immersed in writing mystery, suspense, or romance, she's curled up with a book, devouring everything she can get her hands on.